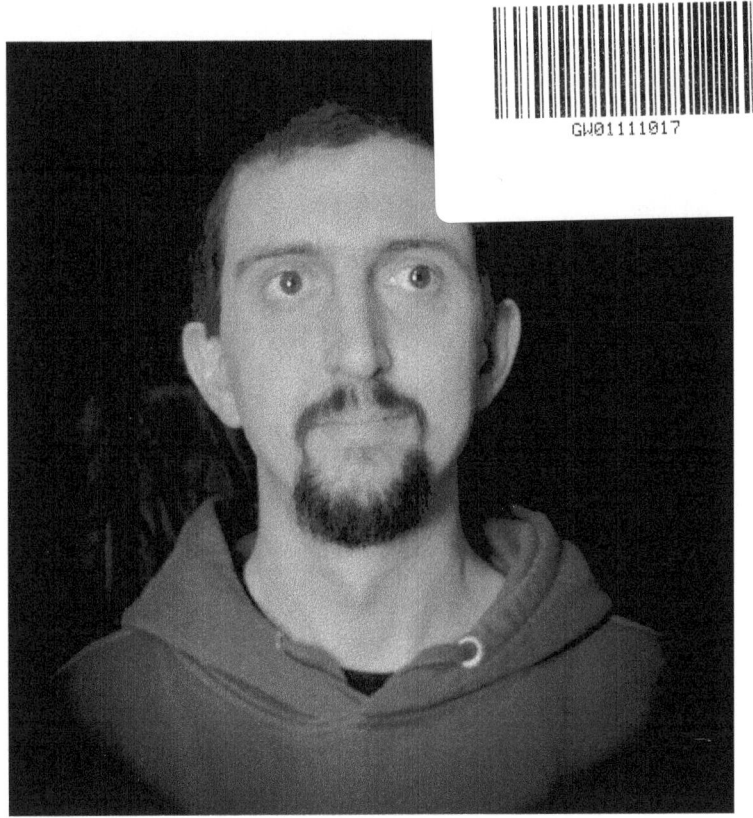

About the Author

Nathan John Franco served for over thirteen years in the United States Army as a Combat Documentation/Production Specialist, or what is more commonly known as a "Combat Cameraman." N.J. Franco has since left the military and now works as a welder for a manufacturing company in Pella, Iowa, United States. He has a wife named Andrea, who is his biggest supporter and motivator, as well as a daughter named Gwendolyn and a son named Joshua. He is also a big fan of fantasy books and draws a lot of his writing inspiration from his favorite author, R.A. Salvatore.

Dathen Legends Book 1: The Immortal War

N.J. Franco

Dathen Legends Book 1: The Immortal War

Olympia Publishers
London

www.olympiapublishers.com
OLYMPIA PAPERBACK EDITION

Copyright © N.J. Franco 2023

The right of N.J. Franco to be identified as author of
this work has been asserted in accordance with sections 77 and 78 of
the Copyright, Designs and Patents Act 1988.

All Rights Reserved

No reproduction, copy or transmission of this publication
may be made without written permission.
No paragraph of this publication may be reproduced,
copied or transmitted save with the written permission of the publisher,
or in accordance with the provisions
of the Copyright Act 1956 (as amended).

Any person who commits any unauthorised act in relation to
this publication may be liable to criminal
prosecution and civil claims for damage.

A CIP catalogue record for this title is
available from the British Library.

ISBN: 978-1-80439-415-1

This is a work of fiction.
Names, characters, places and incidents originate from the writer's
imagination. Any resemblance to actual persons, living or dead, is
purely coincidental.

First Published in 2023

Olympia Publishers
Tallis House
2 Tallis Street
London
EC4Y 0AB

Printed in Great Britain

Preface

Lord Dathro, the newest god to the realm, ruled over the two nations of the Grevanna Province: the Horack nation and the Nairabian nation. Lord Dathro, claiming to be a generous god, openly shared his god-like powers with, at any given time, twelve of his top followers. These top followers were known as "Dathens," and they were able to produce wonderful magical spells, that included being able to hurl balls of fire at their enemies, as well as be able to charge any ordinary weapon with the power of lightning. However, the most impressive spell Lord Dathro gave to his followers was the ability to bring back the dead without so much as a scratch to show for it. His Dathens were free to use their magical abilities as they wished, as long as they followed his rules, known as "Dathen Law." With Lord Dathro's powers being limited to exactly twelve followers, both nations in his province were able to obtain six of the allotted twelve Dathen positions. However, by only having access to exactly half of the generously given powers, neither of the nations had full control over the god-like abilities, causing each nation to feel threatened by the other. This quickly ignited a war between the two nations for ultimate control of the powers, that wouldn't end until one of the two nations came out with twelve Dathens on their side, and the other nation defeated with zero.

Chapter 1

Attack on Rogue's Mountain Keep

The Nairabian army looked like a herd of monstrous turtles as they charged the mountain, because each its warriors carried with them a shield made from the shell of a turtle, known as a 'DyNapus turtle.' The shell was a brownish-green color, with pyramid-shaped studs protruding from it, leaning slightly backwards towards the back of the shell, or what would be considered the bottom of the shield. Each shield was carried above the soldier's head at a forty-five-degree angle, and, when combined with the shields of the surrounding soldiers, formed a blanket-like mass known as a 'Testudo formation.' Therefore, they looked more like a herd of turtles attacking the mountain than they did an army. This style of formation was designed to protect the advancing army from the hail of arrows and boulders that rained down on them from the peaks of the mountain they were charging.

The Nairabians themselves averaged seven feet tall, or more, and were a nation of large, barbarian-like beings, who were accustomed to showing up to battle practically naked, except for a leather waist wrap that was made from the hide of the same monstrous turtle that made up their shields. The Nairabian women who participated in battle had a slight variation to their uniforms from their male counterparts. Along with the same turtle skin waist wrap the men had, the women also wore a similar turtle skin top to cover their chests, to keep them from having to show up to battle topless. Also, all Nairabian warriors, regardless of gender, wore boots made of animal hide.

From atop the mountain stood the opposing force, the Horack nation. The body frame of a typical Horack was smaller in size, by both in height and in muscle, than what you would see from their Nairabian enemies. However, what the Horacks lacked in muscle, they made up for in intelligence. The Horacks were clearly the more technologically advanced of the two nations, being the only army on the battlefield with access to catapults and other artillery weapons. The Horack soldier's battle attire consisted of a yellow, linen shirt, covered by leather breastplate armor, off-white baggy pants, and short boots made of oxen hide.

The black and grey mountain that was being occupied by the defending army was once the home of an ancient thieves' guild, that was eradicated by the Horack nation a few hundred years ago, earning it the name, 'Rogue's Mountain.' Fortunately for the Horacks, there had already been a fortified complex carved straight into the mountain face by its preexisting occupants, that the Horacks could now use against their current enemies, the Nairabians. The Horack nation had also since improved on and expanded its fortifications with additional structures being carved into the rock face. Eight octagon-shaped platforms supported by brick masonry protruded out of the mountain face, forming additional man-made defenses. Each octagonal platform was designed to hold exactly one large catapult and a crew team. Also, about eighty archers stood abreast along each of the walkways between each catapult team, providing additional fire support. This complex of carved rock and man-made structures was known as 'Rogue's Mountain Keep.'

Artilleryman Jonas Milstrum, a member of one of the

catapult fire teams, watched as the Nairabian army moved closer to the mountain. Jonas was considerably tall for a Horack warrior; in fact, if he was a bit stronger, he may have even been able to pass as a Nairabian warrior. Jonas had two crossed ballista bolts tattooed on his right shoulder, as well as the words "Death is not a tragedy, it's just a minor setback" tattooed on his left forearm.

Jonas couldn't possibly have been more bored with the growing situation. He had been in similar situations so many times before, that he had lost all interest, or fear for that matter, of medieval combat. However, the same couldn't be said for Artilleryman Michael Ferns, the newest member of Jonas' team. The fresh-faced warrior had to be at least eighteen years old to join the Horack army, but he honestly looked like he couldn't have been any older than twelve. Artilleryman Ferns was also visibly disturbed by the sight of what was about to commence.

With sweat dripping down his face, Michael Ferns asked, seemingly to no one in particular, "So, uh, um, nobody ever dies in their first battle? Do they?"

Jonas looked at Michael and smirked. "Waker."

'Waker' was a derogatory term that was often used by the more veteran soldiers of the Horack nation. It was used to refer to someone who had never gone through the process of being killed in battle, just to be brought back to life a few days later, like so many of Michael's other brethren had already been accustomed to. The term, while meant to be an insult to the newbie soldier, was still technically true. This was Michael's first-ever battle and therefore, he had not yet had the opportunity to experience such an event.

Another aspect that separated Jonas from Michael, other than their slight age difference, as well as their demeanor towards the battle, was Jonas' uniform had several holes in it, that had been sewn back together. The holes in his uniform had been created from the many battles he had already participated in. Michael's uniform, on the other hand, was still very much whole.

"Alright! Let's make it hail, boys!" Jonas heard his female team leader, Sergeant Erica Stone, suddenly order.

Jonas nodded, took a deep, meditative breath, turned to his right, and faced a large catapult sitting next to him. On his side of the catapult was a large gear with four spokes sticking out of it. He grabbed the top spoke with his left hand, as well as used his right hand to grab another spoke that was sticking out to his right, and started to give the gear a clockwise turn. However, Jonas was met with a moderate amount of resistance upon trying to turn his gear, or at least more resistance than he should have been experiencing. He looked at his new partner, Michael, the warrior on the other side of the catapult, to see what was wrong. Michael was too busy holding a one-thousand-mile stare into oblivion to have any idea what was going on at that moment in time.

"Hey! Waker!" Jonas yelled to his partner.

Michael, snapping back to reality, looked over at Jonas.

"Pay attention," Jonas said in a non-yelling, but still stern voice.

Michael nodded nervously, placed his hands on his own gear of similar design to Jonas', and mimicked the same action Jonas had attempted seconds earlier. Together, Jonas and Michael simultaneously heaved on their respective gears, until each of their gears had completed a one-quarter turn. Once a single quarter-turn had been completed, they then repositioned their hands to complete another turn, making sure to always have at least one hand on a spoke to maintain proper tension. Their turning gears were attached to a wooden beam that had thick, fibrous rope wrapped tightly around it. The ends of those ropes were then tied to another wooden beam that had a metal bucket at the top of it. The turning of the gears rotated the bottom beam, which subsequently pulled on the beam with the metal bucket, pulling it closer to the ground with each turn. This cycle continued until the bucket had moved 90° downwards and had rested leveled with the ground.

There, the third member of the catapult team was waiting in a crouched position. His job was to watch for a small circular ring that was attached to the underside of the metal bucket, to line up with another ring of the same diameter, which was held in place by a small vertical beam adjacent to the bucket. Jonas and Michael, straining from the tension to hold their gears in place, waited for this member of their team to insert a large metal pin through the two rings. Once completed, Jonas and Michael were free to let go of their assigned gears. With the pin in place, this member of the team immediately stepped out of the way to make room for the fourth and final member of the firing team. This member was right on the heels of the previous member and was ready to drop a fifty-five-pound boulder into the readied bucket. The boulder landed in the bucket with a metallic "clang." With the boulder in place, each member of the team then looked at Sergeant Stone for permission to fire.

"Launch it!" she ordered.

The team member whose job it was to place the holding pin, stepped forward again. He grabbed ahold of a small three-foot rope that was attached to a loop on the pin and gave the rope a hardy pull. In the blink of an eye, the pin snapped free, releasing the bucket and its fifty-five pounds of contents.

The boulder hurled towards the Nairabian ranks, which were

still committed to their mountain charge. The boulder landed, striking a Nairabian soldier's raised turtle-shelled shield – fracturing it. The shock of the boulder's impact subsequently shattered the unfortunate warrior's wrist bone. The soldier instinctively dropped his damaged shield and gripped his injured appendage with his free hand. The warrior looked up at the mountain just in time to witness an arrow rocketing towards him, striking him in the eye. The next Nairabian soldier directly behind the now one-eyed warrior crashed into the suddenly stopped soldier and lost his footing. This unfortunate warrior began to fall face-first into the dirt and was quickly skewered by two more arrows that had found their way through the opening in the blanket of shields that had been created by the other soldier's sudden absence. Two more warriors behind that soldier were too close to him to have any chance of avoiding the calamity in progress and both tripped over the fallen warrior's soon-to-be lifeless body. Unable to get back up quick enough, they too were struck by another handful of wooden missiles from above and soon lay bleeding on the battlefield. Fortunately, the soldiers that followed behind the first casualties of the battle were able to avoid being additional members of the spiky, bloody pile-up, and soon picked up their pace to fill in the gap left by the four soldiers. They didn't even stop to walk around their dying comrades; they just charged over the tops of them as if they weren't even there. If the arrows inflicted on the four soldiers hadn't already killed them, the stampede of feet from the one hundred or so soldiers that followed them surely did.

 The Nairabian charge continued amidst the storm of arrows and boulders, with most of the arrows bouncing off their shields unthreateningly. The point of the Horack arrows wasn't to do damage, but instead was to give the Nairabians a reason to keep their shields up, so they couldn't see where the boulders that were raining down on them would land next. Although, it was of course always a bonus when an arrow would make its way through the ranks and strike a soldier, which usually happened immediately after a soldier was taken out by a flying boulder.

The hail of boulders and arrows continued as the Nairabians attempted to survive the gauntlet. Those who didn't survive were just left where they fell. The Nairabians made it to the base of the mountain slope after about ten volleys into the fight. Each soldier then immediately repositioned their turtle-shelled shields in front of them from the forty-five-degree angle they had been at for the first portion of the battle, and began sprinting up the mountain to meet their Horack enemies. The first soldiers to reach the top of the mountain immediately drew out large scimitars from sheathes that were attached to their turtle skin waist wraps. The armed Nairabians immediately began hacking at any unfortunate Horack soldier that got in their way. The Nairabian scimitar was far too large for any Horack soldier to wield properly, but it was almost nothing for the Nairabians with their superior size and strength.

The Horack footmen, brandishing longswords and large wooden shields on their arms, were the first to get into close-quarters combat with their Nairabian enemies that day. The Horack archers that were positioned behind the footmen readied their short sword secondary weapons, knowing they were likely to be entering the fray soon enough. The mixture of carved, as well as man-made structures of the elevated battlefield gave all fighters involved plenty of level ground to stand on, as well as walls to hide behind.

One man attending the battle that day was Sergeant Eric Mac Vaughn, who was likely the bravest and most foolish Horack warrior alive at the time. Excited to get into the mix as quickly as possible, Sergeant Mac Vaughn drew out his longsword and charged at an opponent's unguarded abdomen. The person that Sergeant Mac Vaughn chose to be his first opponent for the battle was Nairabian Footman Wolfgang Ulrich. Footman Ulrich was prepared for Sergeant Mac Vaughn's attack and simply stepped out of the way and then immediately countered it by slicing downwards towards Sergeant Mac Vaughn's exposed neck. Sergeant Mac Vaughn, also quick on his feet, lifted his round shield and stopped the attack. Upon striking the shield, the large scimitar that Footman Ulrich was wielding lodged itself on the outer rim of the wooden equipment, cutting about three inches into it – enough to fully bury the thick blade in the shield.

Sergeant Mac Vaughn and Footman Ulrich were now both attached to each other as long as they both held on to their respective pieces of equipment. While Footman Ulrich wanted to distance himself from Sergeant Mac Vaughn as much as possible, Sergeant Mac Vaughn wanted to pull his opponent in, so he could get control of his enemy's weapon. Sergeant Mac Vaughn took advantage of the closeness between them and landed a short jab with his longsword to the right of Footman Ulrich's abdomen. Sergeant Mac Vaughn smiled evilly at the successful strike. Footman Ulrich, filled with pain and rage, roared as he swung his unobstructed shield at Sergeant Mac Vaughn's head. The force from the hit knocked Sergeant Mac Vaughn to the ground. The blow also freed Sergeant Mac Vaughn's shield and Footman Ulrich's sword from their entanglement, because Footman Ulrich's blade had twisted sideways in the shield and tore a large chunk out of the wooden equipment, freeing his sword.

Sergeant Mac Vaughn had lost his wooden shield on the way down, but he wasn't about to let that stop him from winning the fight. Sergeant Mac Vaughn grabbed an additional longsword that had belonged to one of his fallen friends that he found on the ground, and then quickly got back on his feet to rejoin the duel. Footman Ulrich took his now unobstructed giant scimitar once more and prepared for another strike. Sergeant Mac Vaughn, dual wielding longswords, found a small unguarded opening in Footman Ulrich's abdomen, between his scimitar and his turtle shield. Sergeant Mac Vaughn plunged both his weapons into the soldier's unguarded opening, just as Footman Ulrich's scimitar came careening down on Sergeant Mac Vaughn's neck. No sooner had Sergeant Mac Vaughn's weapons traveled deep enough to puncture his opponent's internal organs, had Sergeant Mac Vaughn's head been completely severed from his body by the oversized scimitar. Sergeant Mac Vaughn's head rolled onto the ground with a euphoric grin still frozen on it. Footman Ulrich may have won the fight, but he too soon bled out from his injuries moments later. If it was possible for the two warriors to still be alive at that moment, they probably would have called it a draw.

    The Nairabian infantry was slaying unfortunate Horack footmen faster than the Horacks could slay them. The Nairabian army broke the Horack battle lines as the Horack's morale dropped.

    A man dressed in the same uniform as the rest of the Horack army watched his struggling comrades from behind the lines. The only difference between his battle attire and the rest of the Horack army present that day was that he was the only Horack soldier on the battlefield that wore a chainmail shirt instead of the leather breastplate, and he also wore a brown satchel that crossed his body diagonally. This man was Hector Vangoff, a Dathen. Not quite a wizard and not quite a paladin, a Dathen was more of a perfect blend of the two classes. Dathen Vangoff was a man in his early thirties with short black hair and patchy facial hair growth.

Dathen Vangoff reached into the brown satchel and pulled out a handful of what mostly appeared to be regular sand, but it wasn't. What made this stuff different than regular old sand was it was coarser. It also seemed to defy physics by having granules with the ability to stick to each other, almost like wet sand, but dry. He cupped his free hand over the mound of sand and started to whisper to it in a peculiar language. As he spoke the words, the sand in his cupped hands began to glow a shade of blue. Seconds later, the man moved his hands apart enough to expose the now blue glowing ball of sand that seemed to levitate in the middle of his hands. However, creating a levitating ball of sand was not the end of the magician's trick. He then secured the blue sand ball with one of his free hands and heaved it like a baseball towards the Nairabian battle lines, making sure to spot an area large enough that was free of Horack allies. The blue ball immediately exploded upon impact with the first warrior it struck! Nairabian warriors were literally blown to pieces and in many cases, flung from the mountainside from the force of the explosion!

Anyone who had ever seen Dathen magic in action knew just how potent that sand really was. However, only those with Dathen training, with an exception to a few others, understood the source of the sand. Both the Nairabian nation and the Horack nation held religious structures inside each of their capital cities that worked as the main headquarters for their respective Dathens. Contained inside these religious buildings, deep underground, were well-like structures that held an unlimited amount of the sand. The religious texts of the two nations claimed that their deity, Lord Dathro, placed those wells there many years ago as a source of his magic for his followers to use. Both the Horack and Nairabian nations had been lucky enough to discover one of the two wells placed randomly throughout the plains of Grevanna, way back when the two nations were still nomadic tribes wandering the grasslands. Once the wells were discovered by the nomadic people, they immediately began constructing their temples around them to keep them protected from their enemies. This then birthed the creation of the nations' two capital cities, Tenton and Hevrog.

    Dathen Vangoff reached into his bag to grab another handful of sand and prepare another spell. He had most of the five pounds of the magical material that had been rationed to him still left in his bag. Furthermore, even if the battle ended with him having an empty bag at his side, he still had barrels of the stuff stored away in his sleeping quarters inside the mountain keep. Barrels of magical sand were often shipped out from the capital city to help support any of the lower-ranking Dathens tasked with combat duty throughout the province. The small team of individuals tasked with supplying the Dathens out in the field with the sand were some of the only non-Dathens in existence to also know about the magical wells of sand. However, they were sworn to secrecy to never speak of the room to any non-Dathens outside their group. The Nairabians also had a similar logistical set up to supply their own Dathens with the sand as well.

    Dathen Vangoff paused while he thought about what he should do with the handful of sand. He wanted to get another Blast Spell off before the enemy advanced too much more, but some of his comrades had moved too close to where the likely blast radius of the explosion would be. He quickly searched his brain for an impromptu alternate spell to use instead. Taking too long to think, a Nairabian footman appeared out of Dathen

Vangoff's left peripheral. The time was now to react. He gripped the sand tightly in his dominant hand and whispered a new incantation. The incoming warrior was almost within striking distance, but it was too late for the Nairabian; the words were already spoken. Dathen Vangoff unclenched his fist and revealed the same sand as before, with the same shade of blue as his previous spell, except it wasn't the same ball shape as before. Instead, it laid as a mound in his hand with an almost paste consistency to it.

Dathen Vangoff tossed the glowing blue sand underhanded, but in an upward motion towards the Nairabian's face. The blue sand turned into a gelatinous consistency in midair and struck the unfortunate warrior in the mouth and lower jaw. A sizzling noise erupted from the Nairabian's face as the magic, gelatinous mass started to burn and melt away his flesh like acid. The wounded Nairabian warrior dropped both his sword and shield as he grabbed his face, wailing in pain, but Dathen Vangoff wasn't done yet. Dathen Vangoff ducked and charged under the lumbering creature who easily had a foot on him, unsheathing his longsword as he went. Without taking the time to look up, he raised his sword straight into the air and hoped to feel the mild resistance of his sword striking flesh.

It did! And the already wounded Nairabian's screams confirmed it. Dathen Vangoff had pierced the Nairabian through the lower jaw and skull. Not taking time to savor the victory, Dathen Vangoff dodged out of the way of the now falling man, who was also still dripping with magic acid mind you, in order to avoid being squashed. One opponent down, Dathen Vangoff disappeared into the fray and continued to fight valiantly, knowing he likely wasn't going to live to see the end of the battle.

For several minutes, the hand-to-hand combat portion of the

battle had stayed localized to the center of the mountain complex. However, the strength of the Nairabians was proving to be too great for the Horack footmen to handle. The Nairabian troops slowly advanced across the east and west masonry bridges that were connected to the eastern and western-most cliffs, which held the majority of the Horack artillery. Jonas, along with the members of his catapult team, as well as the members of the other seven catapult teams, and the archers on the east and west sides of the mountain complex were now in real danger!

Each person, regardless of their primary weapon, whether it was a catapult, or a bow and arrow, immediately discontinued the use of such weapon and drew out their secondary weapon, a short sword. Jonas, being a part of the catapult team on the outermost part of the mountain on the west-side, and therefore one of the furthest people from the action, just waited at the back of the mass of his one hundred or so peers to whittle away enough for him to join in. Suddenly, a small fiery blaze erupted and caught Jonas' eye, followed by another blaze and another. Jonas quickly realized that the other three catapults on the west side of the complex had been set on fire! This was because the Horack army had maintained the policy of burning their artillery weapons in the instance that it looked like they were going to lose a battle. The Horacks believed it was better for their artillery weapons to be destroyed than be in their enemy's hands.

"Light the catapult, Jonas!" Jonas heard Sergeant Stone call.

Jonas nodded in understanding, and without hesitation, he took about two steps towards an unlocked wooden box that was off in a corner of his battle station. He stopped and kneeled down next to the small chest that was barely larger than both his palms put together. He flipped open the box to see a corked glass jar with about twelve ounces of some clear liquid in it, a dingy rag, and a piece of flint rock.

He gathered up the three materials and got to work. Still kneeling, he uncorked the glass jar and set it on the ground. Next, he took the dirty rag and stuffed about half of it into the liquid, making sure enough of it was hanging out of the jar, as to allow a small bit of the rag to be touching the ground. With his short sword still unsheathed, he placed the tip of his blade on the ground at a forty-five-degree angle, about half an inch from where the rag touched the ground. Jonas then took the flint rock and, with a downwards motion, struck the rock against the sharp edge of his blade. Three or four attempts went by, creating little more than a couple of sparks that failed to ignite the rag. Jonas tried again; this time he struck faster and harder than before. A couple of more sparks flew, shortly followed by a sharp pain in Jonas' hand.

Jonas examined his hand to discover a reasonably deep gash in his thumb. Not deep enough to sever his thumb, or even enough for him to lose the use of it, but still deep enough to draw a significant amount of blood. In his haste, Jonas had cut himself on his own blade. Jonas was ready to curse his bad luck; that was until he saw a small flame glowing on the ground next to him. He looked down to get a better view and smiled with glee when he saw that the rag had finally ignited! Ignoring the pain in his hand, he picked up the burning jar and prepared for the final step. He stood with the lit jar still in his hand, now slightly soiled by his own blood, and lightly tossed it underhand at his team's assigned catapult. The jar busted all over the catapult's wooden frame, spilling the clear liquid everywhere, which almost immediately caught fire. Jonas smiled at his success, but it was unfortunately short-lived, as he heard footsteps quickly approaching behind him.

The Nairabian army had managed to chew their way through the rest of the archers and artillerymen that occupied this portion of the base in the amount of time it took Jonas to light his catapult. Now, Jonas and a handful of others were all that was left on this side of the battlefield. Jonas had hoped the footsteps he heard behind him were friendly, but his hopes were in vain when he turned around to discover a large, hulking Nairabian warrior in front of him! Jonas still had his short sword in his hand from when he used it to light the rag, but still didn't have enough time to raise it and try to defend himself with it, before the enemy soldier was able to strike Jonas down with his scimitar. The cut landed on Jonas' right shoulder and cut diagonally across his body until the blade popped out on the other side, just above his left hip. Jonas writhed on the ground just long enough for the excruciating realization to sink in that his upper body was now completely detached from his lower body, and then Jonas' world went dark once more…

Chapter 2

Tenton

A young man, barely past eighteen years of age, was sitting on his designated sleeping cot, clutching a rolled-up piece of parchment. The sleeping cot he sat on was tucked away at the far back wall of a perfectly squared bedroom. The boy's room was made of stone masonry, just like many of the other buildings located in the city. Along the left and right walls of the square room sat two more identical cots. One of the cots belonged to the boy's younger sister, Mika, whose absence from the cot signified that she was already awake. The other cot belonged to his older brother, who hadn't slept in that bed since he moved out nearly five years ago. A small window was positioned at the back of the room, allowing for just enough morning sunlight to come in and illuminate the room.

The teenage boy had beige skin and short, messy black hair, with a thin stubbly beard at the bottom of his lengthy structured face. While still holding the rolled-up parchment, the boy got up, stretched his arms, and walked towards the front door of the bedroom.

Through his bedroom door, he entered a much larger room which worked as a common area for his home, and was also made of stone masonry. Upon entering the common area, the boy could see the only other two rooms in his home. One was the bedroom he just came out of, and the other one was also a bedroom and belonged to the boy's parents, Mortagart and Dillia Milstrum.

An older woman with dark black hair that ran all the way down her back, and a young girl of about twelve years old sat at a large wooden table placed in the center of the common room. The woman was seated at the head of the table and drank juice out of a clay cup, while the young girl was working her way through a bowl of oats. The boy walked across the wooden plank floor, not stopping to join his family at the dining table. He was too focused on the main door of the home to stop and join them for a meal. Instead, he walked past them, and gave them both partially forced pleasantries

"Morning, Mother," he greeted the older woman.

The woman, Dillia, greeted her son back, "Good morning, Enron."

"Morning, Mika," he greeted the younger girl at the table, who, unfortunately, didn't return the greeting as Enron's mother had, but Enron didn't care either.

Enron walked through the front door and immediately entered the residential area of Tenton. Through the dusty streets of the capital city, he initially passed stone masonry houses similarly designed to the one he resided in, until he eventually reached the market area of town. The road he walked on was decorated to his immediate left and right with small, brick buildings, most of them complete with an awning to protect the occupants from the mid-morning sun. Most of the wares sold there consisted of simple food stock, such as flavorless bread, water, and oxen meat, or clothing stores selling simple linen garments. There were also blacksmiths, lots of blacksmiths to supply the Horack army with weapons. Being a nation that had been at war for nearly two hundred years, they had little use for common luxuries. If a profession didn't help the war effort in the slightest, then it was useless.

Enron turned right, down a main road and followed it to 'The Temple', the only religious structure the town had. 'The Temple' was a mostly open courtyard area with a long, rectangular building at its far back. To the left and right of the courtyard area were two, smaller, square buildings. The rectangular building in the back had six windows in it while the other two square buildings remained windowless. Directly in the middle of the courtyard stood a statue of a very young-looking man, and by 'very young', he looked to be in his very late teens at best. The figure in the statue wore what appeared to be a moderately heavy robe and stood in an authoritative posture with his feet spread shoulder width apart and his arms crossed. This man was the Horack's deity, 'Lord Dathro'.

Enron felt the warm brick masonry of The Temple's courtyard under his bare feet, causing him to realize that in his excitement to get to his destination that morning, he had left his home without putting on a proper pair of shoes. Without stopping or slowing his stride, he looked down at his feet to confirm his suspicions that he was indeed shoeless. Enron's momentary distraction left him oblivious to his surroundings and caused him to collide into a fellow pedestrian. The sudden collision brought Enron back to reality long enough for him to stop, turn around, give a quick, forced apology, before he took off running again. He then stopped again three steps into his continued stride and slowly turned around to get a better look at the 'stranger' he had bumped into.

With shock and excitement, Enron spoke, "Jonas?"

Jonas, the same 'Jonas' who had been slain in battle a few days earlier at Rogue's Mountain Keep, now stood before his younger brother, very much alive, and wearing a freshly cleaned, yellow linen shirt and pants, just like the set he had worn the night of the battle. Jonas had once again died in battle, just to be brought back a few days later.

"Brother, what are you doing in Tenton?" Enron asked.

"I could ask you the same thing, Enron," Jonas answered.

"Aren't you supposed to still be at 'Warrior Hill?'"

'Warrior Hill' laid about twelve miles east of Tenton. This was where most of the Horack nation's military personnel went to get their initial training for their assigned job in the Horack army. Despite its name, only the site's barracks were on top of the 'Hill'. The rest of the training site laid at the bottom of the hill and in the surrounding area.

Enron, being the younger sibling, felt compelled to answer his brother's question first. "The answer should be obvious, brother. I have obviously graduated from training and I am ready to be a hero for my beloved nation!" Enron spoke, trying to sound braver than he actually was.

"Hero, huh?" Jonas laughed. "Tell me again, what is my 'hero' brother's role in this fight?"

Enron took a deep breath, sighed, paused for another second, and then answered as proudly as he could, "Footman." Although, he was not at all pleased with his assigned position.

Jonas scoffed. "Well that figures! You have no skills, no ambition in life." Jonas shrugged his shoulders and then rhetorically asked, "What else are you good for?"

Enron was hurt by his brother's comment, but he also knew Jonas was right. Enron was never sure what he wanted out of life and now he was stuck with the hand he had been dealt by the ruling council.

"Fine!" Enron spoke angrily, still hurt by his brother's blunt honesty. "I told you why I'm here. Why are you here?"

Jonas sighed, "Come on, brother, don't be such a 'Waker'. You saw me walking out of The Temple. Why do you think I'm here?" Jonas answered.

Without waiting for Enron to say any more, Jonas turned around and left.

Enron, confused by the new, and assumingly insulting term, asked, "Hey! Jonas! What's a 'Waker?'"

Jonas, without turning around or even stopping, answered his brother, "Don't worry, you'll find out soon enough. Everyone finds out eventually."

Enron decided to let the definition of the new term remain unknown for now. Enron was just about ready to continue his journey to his destination, but ran into yet another familiar, but this time unfortunate face. The man was George Grook, a short, stout, older man, with a shaved head that was adorned with rune-like tattoos. The tattoos were written in a language that only a Dathen, or a Dathen in training could understand. The Dathens, believe it or not, had their own language that was created by their deity, 'Lord Dathro'. It was this language that the ancient religious texts were written in, and it was also this language the Dathens spoke in when casting their spells. Despite only seven living Horacks being able to read the language, the tattoo on Dathen Grook's head contained the names of all the units he served with during his time as a Dathen Battle Mage many years ago. Dathen Grook secretly missed the old days of his time in combat. He liked being on the front lines of the war and fighting alongside the other heroes of his nation.

However, something that was unfortunate about being a Dathen, or fortunate, depending on how you looked at it, was the fact that just about every Dathen was destined to level up to a higher position at some point in their career. There were no less than six certified Dathens, as well as an additional Dathen Apprentice in the Horack army at any given time. The first title you held as a certified Dathen was called 'Dathen Battle Mage'. They were the ones on the front lines of battle, casting the damage-dealing spells and fighting off their Nairabian enemies. Three of the six certified Dathens held this position in their society. After 'Dathen Battle Mage', came 'Dathen Guardian'. For this position, there were always exactly two of them at any given time in the Horack nation, and it was their job to stay behind in Tenton and do the majority of the raising of the fallen warriors after a battle. It was also their job to protect the one person holding the third and final title: 'Dathen Lord'. The Dathen Lord was the oldest of the Dathen crew and was known to be the keeper of the ancient religious text, knowledge, and history of their religion. There was also, of course, the title of 'Dathen Apprentice'. While not a certified Dathen yet, they were the one person being trained by the other six Dathens to one day become an actual Dathen.

Upon a Dathen's death, either by old age or some other natural cause, other than falling in battle, the remaining members of the Dathen clan would then be promoted up the chain to the next rank. This was also the point where the chosen Dathen Apprentice would officially become a certified Dathen and move from Apprentice to Dathen Battle Mage. The newly updated Dathen team would also take this time to pick themselves a new Apprentice to start training, and therefore, continuing the cycle of always having six Dathens and an Apprentice.

Some Dathens from years past may have looked towards their promotion from Dathen Battle Mage to Dathen Guardian as a good thing, because it was a good opportunity to get away from the pain and horror of battle. However, Dathen Grook was not one of those people. For Dathen Grook, taking him away from the battlefield he loved had just turned him into a bitter old man.

"What are you doing here, boy?" Dathen Grook spoke in the deep, gravelly voice he was known for. Dathen Grook didn't even give poor Enron a chance to answer the now rhetorical question. "This building is only for the Dathens and the dead. You certainly aren't a Dathen, and, well, as far as being dead, you look like you've gone your entire life without getting so much as a paper cut." Dathen Grook laughed.

"Alright, Georgie, be nice." A much more calm and friendly voice came from behind Dathen Grook.

Dathen Grook gave a mild gasp under his breath and then gave a sideways glance at the source of the newest member to the conversation. Dathen George Grook hated being called 'Georgie', but unfortunately for him, this time the name-calling came from one of the only people who could call him that and get away with it. It was Enron's father, Mortagart Milstrum.

Mortagart was taller than Enron, but was still shorter than his eldest son, Jonas. He had short, salt and pepper hair, circular eyeglasses, and a 'soul patch' style beard that was about an inch wide and extended from the bottom of his lip, to curling around slightly under his chin, with a faint line of grey running directly down it. In general, Mortagart looked more like his eldest son Jonas, tall and handsome, than he did his youngest son, Enron. Mortagart, being a Dathen Guardian as well, was a colleague of Dathen Grook. The only difference between Dathen Grook and Dathen Milstrum was that Dathen Grook had been a Dathen longer than Dathen Milstrum, which meant he was the next in line to become the Dathen Lord, once Dathen Lord Gabriel Benedict passed away. After that, in the instance of Dathen Lord Grook then dying, Dathen Guardian Milstrum would then take his place as the Dathen Lord.

"Dad!" Enron exclaimed.

"Enron," Mortagart answered his son. "What brings you here?" Mortagart asked. "And without proper footwear," noting his son's bare feet.

Enron shuffled his feet, trying to hide each of his feet behind the other foot, but this of course was impossible. Giving up, he held up the rolled parchment he had carried all the way from his home and did his best to explain his intentions, but his embarrassment over his lack of footwear caused his words to fail him. "I, um, have to, uh, report, for…"

Looking at the parchment his son was holding, Mortagart was able to easily conclude what his son was trying to get at and said, "Oh, right. Of course. Well, son, I'll let you be on your way. Don't forget to spend some time with your sister while you're here, and with your brother. You probably don't know yet, but he is in town too for the night."

Enron, not having time to chat, politely dismissed himself and walked off in the direction of Tenton Keep, which was still a couple of more blocks away.

Enron smirked at the fact that his father was unaware that he had already seen his brother that day.

Tenton Keep primarily consisted of a large, rectangular structure, with five defense towers in it. Four of the defense towers dotted each of the four corners of the rectangular building, while the fifth one was positioned slightly off-center from the front of the building, next to the gatehouse. These towers were, at this point in the Horack nation's history, mostly there for aesthetics. The city of Tenton already had a defensive wall around its perimeter, that, if the enemy forces were to ever breach it, there was very little Tenton could do to further stop them. Even with the assistance of the keep, Tenton would likely fall. The five towers did once serve a defensive purpose early in the Horack nation's history, back when Tenton comprised mostly of the main keep and a few dozen houses. However, the towers became obsolete once the town wall was added about a hundred years ago.

The keep's gatehouse was a brick structure with a crude walking path of randomly placed stones leading up to it. The gatehouse was also constructed to include a portcullis, a grate-like feature that could be raised or lowered for the defense of the keep. This was another nearly obsolete mechanism from early in the Horack nation's history.

The brick structure that was officially known as 'Tenton Keep' now served mostly as a weapon storage facility as well as a barracks for the soldiers assigned to Tenton for the city's defense. There were also several workshops, as well as additional blacksmith shops that surrounded the main keep. The largest building, other than the keep itself, stood behind it and served as storage for the Horack army's unused catapults and other artillery weapons. The building itself was made of wood, and its attic had been filled with straw, as a way to quickly ignite and dispose of the weapons contained within it in case the city was taken over. This was yet another precaution the Horacks took to ensure the Nairabians never got a hold of their much sought-after artillery weapons.

Enron approached the keep's gatehouse, where two Horack footmen with longswords stood guard.

"Hold up there," one of the guards immediately spoke. "What's your authorization?"

Enron cowered his head low and handed the intimidating man the rolled parchment he had brought from home. The guard snatched it out of Enron's hand, unrolled it, and looked over it. The parchment read:

Enron Milstrum,
You are hereby granted a 24-hour stay in your hometown, Tenton, to gather a few personal belongings and to get any affairs in order you that deem necessary. By 0900 on September 1st, you are to report to Tenton Keep for an equipment fitting and further instructions on your first assignment. The following morning, September 2nd, you are to meet at Tenton Keep once more to begin your march to your first assignment at Outpost Scorpion in the Pastoria Province of the Grevanna Grasslands.
Respectfully,
Logistics Sergeant MacBeth.

The guard stopped partway through his reading to eyeball Enron, who was nervously waiting for the ordeal to be over. The guard then shifted the document over to his partner so he could see the letter, making sure to point at a particular word on the paper. What that word was, Enron couldn't tell. Whatever it was, it made the second guard snicker. The first guard then pulled the document back towards him and tossed it at Enron, hitting him in the face. The first guard then motioned with his head as well as his right-hand thumb, signaling that Enron was authorized to proceed into the keep.

Enron entered the brick gatehouse of the keep and was immediately met with a wooden sign hanging from the wall. On the sign, the word 'Armory', as well as an arrow pointing left, was drawn on it in white paint. Enron looked to his left to see that there was indeed a door there, just as the sign suggested. Enron immediately walked through the door without hesitation.

The next room Enron entered was significantly larger than the last. It was a massive, rectangular room with a long counter that ran the length of it. A black-haired woman dressed in a Horack soldier's uniform, minus any weaponry or protective equipment, stood on the opposite side of the counter as Enron. Behind her was a double door that had one of its two doors propped open. The room was lit with torches hanging from the walls that seemed to not emanate smoke of any kind. The smokeless torches that hung in the room were actually created by a low-level Dathen spell. Not only did they not emit any smoke, to keep any occupants in the room from suffering from smoke inhalation in such a close-quarters environment, but the magic torches were also guaranteed to burn consistently for exactly twenty-four hours. On Enron's side of the room, there was also a series of windows positioned every few feet on the wall. These windows, combined with the smokeless torches, illuminated the hall-like room well enough for its occupants to operate in. It wasn't perfect lighting, but it was sufficient.

Enron gazed hard at the smokeless torches. He had heard his father speak of them when he was younger, but he had never actually seen them before. His father had also told him that the torches generated a warm heat that wouldn't burn your skin if touched.

Enron's father would tell him, "You could literally put your entire hand into the flame of the torch, and it wouldn't hurt except for a mild warming sensation."

Enron, knowing his father would never lie to him about such a thing, reached up to touch the flame of one of the nearby torches. The torch did feel warm, just like his father told him it would. Overwhelmed by curiosity, as well as a rare stroke of braveness, Enron inched his hand closer to the flame, wanting to touch it.

"Can I help you?" the female soldier called out to Enron with an annoyed tone in her voice.

Enron, caught off guard by the sudden interruption, quickly snatched his hand away from the flame, ending his experiment. Enron, not wanting to upset the already annoyed woman any further, broke into a light jog down the long room to where she waited for him.

"Name?" the woman spoke.

"Oh, um." Enron swallowed hard and then softly squeaked, "Enron Milstrum."

"Right, stay there," the female soldier sternly spoke with the same tone of voice. She then momentarily crouched down, disappearing behind the long counter before reappearing again a moment later. When she reappeared, she had with her a pile of folded clothing, topped with two pairs of oxen hide, high top shoes. The pile contained two pairs of long, off-white linen pants, two pairs of long-sleeved yellow linen shirts, two pairs of short-sleeved yellow linen shirts, and of course the two pairs of oxen hide, high top shoes.

"Alright, now move down to the other end of the counter to get your gear," the female soldier ordered.

Enron obeyed her order and walked about twelve paces to his left, until he came across another weaponless soldier. This time it was a man with a thin scruffy beard and thick black hair. However, this man chose to not say anything to Enron. Instead, as soon as Enron appeared before him, the man turned around and grabbed a random longsword off a rack of swords behind him, as well as an olive-green round shield from a pile of shields that sat next to the rack. The man handed the weapon and shield to Enron. Enron smiled as he inspected the far from brand new equipment. The blade had a small dent running down the middle of it, but other than that, it was still a perfectly usable sword.

Most importantly, the edge of the blade had been freshly sharpened. This slightly used blade was still considered to be a major upgrade from the weapon he had been given at Warrior Hill for training.

Enron was initially given a wooden sword to train with before being trusted with a real one. Even the real blade he was given for training purposes was still worse than his current one. That blade he had been given for training was very dull and even had chunks of metal missing from the blade's edge. That sword probably couldn't cut through paper, much less a person. Enron's current shield also showed signs of previous usage, but again, it was still an improvement from the training shield he had been given at Warrior Hill. There were small scratches here and there along the front of it, but the largest mark of damage was of a triangular-like wedge that had been chopped into the outer rim of the shield that was then was hastily patched up with a similarly shaped piece of scrap wood. Whoever repaired this shield didn't even bother taking the time to paint the scrap of wood to match the rest of the shield. Enron, without hesitation or further instruction from the weapons clerk in front of him, took his new gear and walked off.

"Hold up there, 'hero'," Enron heard the weapons clerk utter sarcastically.

Enron turned around to see what the man wanted. Enron immediately noticed the man holding a leather breastplate, a belt, and a sword sheath in his hands. The clerk held up the equipment as if to suggest, "Did you forget something?" Enron, realizing what the man wanted, slowly and shamefully walked back to him to get the rest of his gear. With all his gear finally in hand, as well as some additional official documents being signed upon his receipt of the equipment, Enron ran home to try his new gear on.

Busting through the front door of his home, Enron greeted his mother and sister instinctively with a "Hi, Mom, hi, Mika," but he didn't even stop to see if they were even home. As far as he knew, he may have been speaking to an empty room, but he didn't care either.

Inside his room, Enron examined his new clothes. Something he noticed about them that he didn't see the first time the clerk handed them to him were the words, "E. Milstrum" embroidered on a cloth tag on the inside of his shirts and pants. The shirts, both the short-sleeves and the long-sleeves had the tag located on the inside of the shirt, near the bottom, where his left hip would be. The pants had their tag in a similar location, except they were at the top of the pants, again, where the left hip would be. Enron shrugged it off as nothing he should worry too much about. After all, its purpose was obvious. They were meant to mark the clothes as being his. "E. Milstrum" meaning his name "Enron Milstrum." As Enron began to get dressed, he noticed, "E. Milstrum" was also embroidered into one more piece of clothing. This time it was around the inside neck of both sets of his issued footwear.

Finally, fully dressed, he stood in front of his floor mirror and admired himself. He had spent that last year of his life being very displeased with the decision of the council for him to be a footman, but now, seeing himself as a trained fighter in a soldier's uniform, he had never been prouder of himself. Enron drew out his sword and began wailing it around, working through some of the attack drills he had learned at Warrior Hill. Holding his round shield with the top of it at shoulder height, Enron practiced the same two repetitive strikes over and over. First a high jab in an uppercut fashion, designed specifically as an attack against the Horack's taller enemies, the Nairabians. The jab's purpose was to skewer their opponents through the lower jaw and skull. The second-strike Enron practiced was also a jab attack, but it was a lower attack meant to hit their opponents in the gut. High jab, mid jab, he practiced over and over until he heard a familiar young girl's voice behind him.

"What are you doing?" his younger sister, Mika, asked.

Enron, startled by the unexpected voice, dropped his weapon on the ground.

"My hero," his sister sighed. This was the second time in the past twenty minutes he had been called 'hero' in a sarcastic and demeaning tone.

Enron sighed when he realized it was his sister that had interrupted his sword practice. He quickly picked his dropped sword off the ground and turned to face his sister, and asked, "What are you doing here?"

"What am I doing here?" she repeated, "In my room? I live here, remember? Speaking of which, when are you leaving again? Tomorrow?"

"What's your hurry to see me go?" Enron inquired.

"Look, I've been sharing my room with two smelly older brothers for the past twelve years and I am looking forward to finally having a room to myself."

"Oh, Mika, you know you love us," Enron teased.

Mika sighed and teased back, "Yes, as your sister, I love you, but that doesn't mean I can tolerate you."

Enron smiled at his sister and left the room, patting her on her shoulder-length brown hair as he went. Upon entering the main room of his home, Enron was met by the shrill voice of his mother scolding him, "ENRON MAURICE MILSTRUM! DON'T YOU DARE THINK ABOUT COMING TO THE BREAKFAST TABLE WITH THAT SWORD AND ALL THAT

ARMOR ON!"

Enron shocked by his mother's outburst, turned on his heels and went straight back into his room to take off his sword and leather armor. Enron reentered the main room moments later with just his uniform on, similarly to how the two clerks he met at Tenton Keep were dressed. Enron sat down at the table that occupied the center of the room and began to nibble on a piece of toasted bread that had since gone cold.

Enron spent the rest of his granted stay in Tenton with his family. He was originally expected to only get to spend time with his father, mother, and sister, but the unexpected arrival of his older brother, Jonas, was definitely considered to be a bonus for him. For dinner that night, Enron's mother made a special meal of ox steaks and potatoes with a glass of melon juice to drink.

The dining area of Enron and his family's brick home was illuminated with simple, non-magical candles that emitted smoke like regular candles would. The fact of the matter was the town Temple and Tenton Keep were the only buildings in the city that were authorized to have magically created, smokeless torches in them, like Enron had seen earlier that day. Every morning, the city's designated Dathen Apprentice would wake up and perform one of the few spells they were allowed to perform, the Smokeless Torch Spell, to light the torches of both Tenton Keep and The Temple. The Dathen Apprentice was far too busy with the rest of his Dathen training to be able to stop by every single house and building in the city to cast the same spell for the residents and would just skip the other establishments in the city – leaving the residents to light their homes by more traditional means.

Enron's father, of course, knew the magical incantation needed to perform the same Smokeless Torch Spell; all he needed was a torch or similar medium to set the magical fire to, as well as a handful of the magical sand component. However, Dathen Law stated that Dathen magic was strictly forbidden to be used for personal pleasures. One of the earliest Dathen Lords in their nation's history, Dathen Lord Hempwood, interpreted the sacred texts that made up the Dathen Laws as to mean that Dathens couldn't use this particular spell inside their homes. The Dathen Lords that proceeded Dathen Lord Hempwood then continued with the tradition after his inevitable passing.

Enron thoroughly enjoyed his time with his family, for he had no idea how long it would be before he would get to see them again. Whenever Enron made any comments about the uncertainty of his next Tenton visit, his brother Jonas was always sure to laugh it off and say, "Don't worry, you'll probably be back here again in a couple of months." Jonas of course was only half-joking whenever he said this, but Enron had no idea how right his brother actually was.

Chapter 3

The Journey North

Enron walked through the streets of his hometown, taking the same route to Tenton Keep he had taken the day prior. The sun had just begun to rise in the east just enough to paint the sky in a vibrant blend of pink, yellow, and gold, thus providing Enron with just enough low light for him to navigate the streets safely, without the aid of torchlight. Enron, dressed in his military uniform and combat gear, strutted proudly the whole way.

At the Keep, Enron was quickly shuttled into two formations, totaling forty-eight people, with each formation consisting of six rows of four. Enron immediately recognized many of the soldiers in the two formations with him, for he had trained with many of them at Warrior Hill. Enron spent time exchanging pleasantries and small talk with a couple of his peers from 'The Hill', until a much older man approached the group and moved towards the front of the formation. He was a tall man, with almost completely white hair except for just a couple of specks of grey still left. The man's face was also completely free of any facial hair, which was considered to be a slightly abnormal fashion choice for the older generation of Horack men.

"Good morning," the man spoke in a low, tired voice. "I am Master Sergeant Gillman, and I will be your guide to Pastoria this morning."

After a quick gear check and an issuing of provisions for the day, the four dozen soldiers began their march for the Tenton front gate. Local shop keepers could be seen opening their businesses for the day as the soldiers passed, but the merchants paid them little attention, because a couple of troop formations marching through town was not an uncommon occurrence in Tenton. The massive thirty-foot door that was the Tenton front gate was already open upon their arrival. It was usually opened by the early morning shift gate guards upon the first sign of morning sunlight coming over the horizon and usually stayed open during the daylight hours for the inbound and outbound traffic. It would then be closed again for the night by the night shift gate guards once they saw the last bit of sunlight had disappeared for the day. The Tenton front gate could also be quickly shut at any point if a possible attack was spotted by any of the guards in the watchtowers that dotted the perimeter wall.

The soldiers marched straight out of the Tenton front gate and into the open landscape of the Grevanna Grasslands. The morning sun had completely risen above the horizon, ceasing the colorization in the clouds it had created an hour earlier. Upon exiting the gate, the two formations were immediately met by two additional formations who were already waiting for them. While Enron and the two formations he was a part of were all footmen, these two new formations consisted exclusively of archers.

"Morning, Master Sergeant Gillman! Glad you could join us, old man. We were getting ready to leave without ya!" A younger-looking soldier, also a master sergeant, jokingly spoke to his peer. This new Master Sergeant wasn't as old as Master Sergeant Gillman, but was still an older-looking gentleman, with a nice sprinkling of salt and pepper hair. This man was Master Sergeant Jarum and he oversaw the two archery formations. Master

Sergeant Gillman, upon seeing his peer, walked up to him and gave him a firm handshake. The four groups of soldiers reformed into a larger formation, with the two footmen formations led by Master Sergeant Gillman in the front, followed by the two archery formations led by Master Sergeant Jarum in the back.

The ninety-six soldiers marched northward out of Tenton towards their final destination, Pastoria. Enron wanted nothing more but to continue to catch up with the friends he had made while training at Warrior Hill, but unfortunately, there was absolutely no talking allowed while marching in formation. This was partially to maintain a certain level of discipline expected from a Horack soldier, but most importantly, it was to help keep the noise pollution low enough to avoid being heard by any enemies in the area as they marched. It was very unlikely that the marching troops would come across any hostile forces this far into Horack nation, but one could never be too careful. The truth of the matter was, the ninety-six-member strong formation would likely be easily decimated by any Nairabians in the area that wished to do them harm.

Not even thirty minutes into their march and Enron had already begun to break a sweat from walking. Enron had been trained to endure long foot marches while he trained at Warrior Hill, but that didn't mean he enjoyed them any more than he had before he started his training. Most of his sweat collected around his chest and back area due to the trapped body heat from his leather breastplate armor. Enron took a couple of swigs of water from his water skin to help keep him cool. Enron wanted to chug the entire water skin right then and there, but he knew it was better for him to conserve the amount of water that had been rationed to him.

The soldiers stopped for lunch about four hours into their

trek. Both Master Sergeant Gillman and Master Sergeant Jarum had worked in concert to form the soldiers into two circular formations, off to the side of the road that they had been marching on. The infantry soldiers formed an outer perimeter of defense around the archery platoons who then formed their own inner perimeter of defense. Each soldier, regardless of profession, crouched into a kneeling position to enjoy their lunch of field bread and ox jerky, while they maintained security. They also had received in their daily ration, a couple of pieces of a strange root that Enron had never seen before. The new food was small and resembled ginger root, except it was a dirt-brown color. Although Enron had never officially seen this item before, he had definitely heard his older brother Jonas talk about it before. The food items were referred to as 'Doroots'. They were a common field ration among the Horack military and were known for their ability to retain water, thus, they were used as a means to feed the troops as well as keep them hydrated.

    Enron picked up a small piece of Doroot with his fingers and noticed it had a slightly moist texture to it. Enron then placed the food item in his mouth and began to chew it with his back molars. The look of disgust on Enron's face must have been priceless as he immediately regretted his decision to eat this alien food. To him, it tasted like a piece of chewy, waterlogged wood. Enron quickly spat the partially chewed morsel back into his hand and placed it back into his field bag that had contained the rest of his food. Enron decided he would rather stay hydrated from his issued water skin, than eat another piece of that disgusting root. The fifteen-minute lunch break passed quickly, and it was once again time for the troops to get back up and resume the foot march.

    The second half of their march was just as long and boring

as the first half. For Enron and his fellow troops, there wasn't much for them to look at. It was mostly grassy fields dotted with trees, which was consistent with the rest of Grevanna. There was also an occasional mountain or hill off in the distance to look at. However, things began to take a slightly more interesting turn during the last hour of Enron's march. It was at this point in the trek that he began to see something new off in the distance. It was some sort of civilization that Enron had never seen before. Enron wasn't able to see much at first, but he was able to make out some sort of man-made dirt walls that had been built up around the civilization. The walls were green in color from being overgrown with wild plant vegetation over the years. Unfortunately, Enron couldn't see much beyond that, because the walls were simply too high for him to make out any form of additional structures inside the established civilization. This alien town was Pastoria, a rural farmland environment that was where the majority of the Horack's meat and plant-based foods came from.

 Master Sergeant Gillman and Master Sergeant Jarum both marched their respective troops through an opening in the perimeter walls, that made up the front entrance to the complex. This space in the perimeter was lightly guarded by two armed soldiers, who sported the same gear as Enron: a single longsword and a large, wooden round shield. Without hesitation or asking any questions, the two guards stepped out of the way of the marching troops to allow them to enter the civilization. One of the two soldiers was an older gentleman and appeared to be in a bad mood at the time. The other one was slightly older than Enron, but was still younger and appeared happier than his guard partner.

 As the troops marched through the front gate, the younger guard greeted the formations. "Welcome to Pastoria!"

***

Pastoria spanned for many miles to the north, east, and west, with every mile of the perimeter being protected by the same dirt wall. Enron had always known Pastoria existed, but he had never seen anything like it before. For one thing, there was more green, lush vegetation here than he had seen anywhere else. Although there was still a good deal of wild grass and trees to be seen, like everywhere else in Grevanna, there were additional domesticated plants and trees, too, such as cornfields, wheat fields, apple orchards, and vineyards.

Enron and his company traveled down a dirt path that led from the front entrance of the complex, where they had met the two gate guards earlier. As the formations marched, they could see farmers that were dressed in dirty work clothes pulling weeds and harvesting a variety of fruits, vegetables, and berries. Enron could also see many cattle farmers herding oxen. Ox was the main meat staple for the Horack nation, but there were also several chicken farms as well. It was also not just adults that Enron saw at work, but children as young as ten were seen running around the fields, chasing cattle and chickens into organized masses. There was also the unfortunate smell of fresh manure that hung in the air that made Enron want to gag as he breathed it in.

The troops marched on for about another three miles, until they began to see another compound inside the larger fortification they were already in. The perimeter wall of this new place had been constructed from built-up loose dirt, just like the perimeter wall they saw when they first entered Pastoria. It even had grown vines and other wild plant life on it from over the years, just like the perimeter wall that surrounded Pastoria. Several wooden watchtowers that extended high above the dirt wall could also be spotted just inside the compound. For now, that was all Enron could see, for the dirt walls were far too high to expose much of the inside. This secondary compound was known as 'Outpost Scorpion'.

Once inside, Enron could see that the internal structures of the compound were made mostly of stone, but they weren't like the manufactured bricks used to build Tenton Keep, or the other homes and businesses in Tenton. These were literal stones – rocks that were harvested from a nearby mountain named 'The Queen Maria Mountain', also nicknamed 'The Mountain of the Three Queens', because of how three of its peaks stuck up to look like three queens standing together.

Enron's formation continued down yet another footpath until they came to a building that had been built out of smooth brick masonry, unlike the rough rock masonry that made up the other structures inside the compound. The formation abruptly turned right upon reaching this new building and down the final footpath they would take before they would reach their intended destination. They soon arrived at a dozen or so identical, rectangular buildings set up in a row. These were the Outpost Scorpion barracks. Each soldier was then systematically assigned to a different barrack building. Most of the guys were assigned to a building wherever there happened to be room. However, the twenty-three females in the group were all put into the same barracks together at the far end of the barracks line. Some could say it was a coincidence that they all ended up in the same building, but not really. There were only four female barracks, so odds were that most, if not all of them would end up together in the same barracks.

The insides of the barracks, regardless if they were male or female, were all the same: each barracks contained exactly sixty cots lining the walls, thirty on each side. In front of each cot was a small locking chest for the occupant's personal items. The barracks, for the most part, at least the male barracks, were quite a mess. Enron walked into his assigned building to see cots unmade and gear strewn about every which way. Many off-duty Horack soldiers could be seen sleeping or sitting on their bed in some dressed down variation of their uniform, talking with their neighbors or playing cards. This marked the beginning of Enron's new life as a soldier in Pastoria.

Chapter 4

Scheming

Inside a castle chamber, inside the Nairabian Capital of Hevrog, two men stood examining a map that was spread out on a table. The room contained several torches along one wall that were powered by the same Dathen spell that allowed for the torches of the Horack nation to be smokeless, as well as run for a twenty-four-hour period. There was also a roaring fire set in a fireplace in the center of the same wall as the torches, and just like the magic torches along the wall, this fireplace didn't emit any smoke and was guaranteed to run for twenty-four hours straight. Although, the fireplace did still act like an actual fireplace in the sense that it generated a warming sensation whenever anyone got near it. It even crackled and popped like a real fireplace. There were also glass windows along the opposite wall, as well as an opened door hatch on the ceiling to let sunlight in that could be closed and locked from the inside as needed. In a world where electricity didn't exist, every precaution had been taken to ensure maximum illumination for this chamber, for this was the Nairabian War Room.

The eldest of the two men was Grand Marshal Eric Ratlin, and at six feet eight inches tall, he was the average height for a Nairabian male. Despite being 'average' in height, he still took full advantage of his Nairabian heritage to bulk up and strengthen his body to make himself as intimidating as possible, both to his enemies as well as to his rivals. Grand Marshal Ratlin also had a grey and black tattoo of a skull surrounded by smoke on his right shoulder. The second man in the room was Colonel Allen Blackridge, who was younger and appeared to be in his late thirties. He was a tall man, even by Nairabian standards, at a whopping eight feet two inches tall. He had a full beard that came together into a double braided goatee on his chin. Both men were dressed in their turtle skin waist wraps that made up the majority of their standard-issue Nairabian military uniforms, though both of the men were also weaponless at the time.

"Sir, are you proposing that we attack the Horack capital, DURING A FUNERAL?" Colonel Blackridge exclaimed, clearly not happy about the idea.

"Exactly," Grand Marshal Ratlin slyly answered back, as if the suggested deed was completely normal.

The front door of the castle chamber then creaked open and Dathen Lord Dante Danathan stepped in. Dathen Lord Danathan had short, solid white hair, which was typical of a man of his title. However, a trait that wasn't typical of past Dathen Lords was the fact that his face was completely clean-shaven, as well as that he did not look to be the typical age of a Dathen Lord, other than his white hair. He claimed to be ninety years old, but the number of wrinkles and other aging imperfections in his face and skin suggested he couldn't be any older than fifty. Nairabian Dathens and Dathen Lords weren't particularly known for their muscular physique, in comparison to your typical Nairabian footman, but they did still maintain a certain level of muscle tone, as they still had Nairabian blood running through their veins, and Dathen Lord Danathan was no different in that aspect.

"What are you two scheming now?" Dathen Lord Danathan asked the two Nairabian officers, with a clear annoyance in his voice.

"Sir, we're 'scheming' a plan to finally end this war," Grand Marshal Ratlin answered his boss.

"Well, Grand Marshal Ratlin, tell me, what is this grand plan of yours?" Dathen Lord Danathan asked in a doubtful tone.

"Well," Grand Marshal Ratlin smiled evilly, "sir, I think everyone would agree that the only way to win this war is to completely eliminate all Dathens on the opposing side. You eliminate the Dathens, you eliminate their ability to bring back their warriors once we kill them. From there, it's just a matter of time before we kill enough of their warriors without them coming back before the Horacks surrender."

"Yes, Ratlin, we know this. Everyone over the age of five has realized this technicality by now. What's your point?" Dathen Lord Danathan fumed.

"My point is, sir, I may have finally realized the perfect opportunity for us to implement this assumed plan."

Dathen Lord Danathan crossed his arms, looking angrier by the second. He then freed one of his crossed arms and gestured for the Grand Marshal to continue explaining his plan.

Grand Marshal Ratlin smiled at Dathen Lord Danathan's discomfort and was happy to continue. "Well, it's like this, sir. The Horack's Dathen Lord, Dathen Lord Gabriel Benedict, is old. He's older than any other Dathen Lord has managed to live to, that we know of, and reports claim that he is pushing a hundred and three years old. So, all we have to do is wait for the crusty old man to croak, and we will swoop in to make our attack on the capital. As you know, sir, once he dies of old age, all other Dathens in the Horack nation, to include whoever they pick as their new apprentice, will be called back to the capital to attend the funeral. This will be our best opportunity to kill all six of their

Dathens and their apprentice all at once, because they won't be allowed to bring back their deceased Dathen Lord. As you also know sir, it is forbidden by Dathen Law to use resurrection magic to bring back anyone who dies of old age or illness."

"Yes, yes, Ratlin, I know what the law says. No one knows Dathen Law better than I do!" Dathen Lord Danathan interrupted, before pausing momentarily to contemplate his next move. Finally, an idea on how to defeat the Grand Marshal's proposed plan came to him.

"Fine," the Dathen Lord began, "the old man will die soon, but we don't know when. Unfortunately, once the old man croaks, it will take a week for us to catch word of his death, and then another week to gather the troops together to march them across the open plains to the capital. By then, everyone would have cleared out and your plan will fail."

Grand Marshal Ratlin smiled again, happy to have his rebuttal already planned out. "Sir, that's why I sent out three brigades nearly a week ago to be set up near the Horack capital. The brigades will remain far enough away from the city to avoid being seen, and each day they will send out scouting parties to keep an eye on the front gate of the capital to watch for an increased volume of traffic entering the city. Once that happens, it can be assumed the Dathen Lord is dead. That is when we will make our attack. Also, sir, we have reinforcements coming in from the north that have been redirected to join them. We will certainly have more than enough troops to take the city!"

Dathen Lord Danathan opened his mouth to say something, but nothing came out. Instead, he groaned, turned around, and stormed out of the chamber through the same door he entered in.

Colonel Allen Blackridge leaned over next to Grand Marshal Ratlin as the Nairabian elder exited, and whispered, "You know,

I get the feeling that he really doesn't like you very much, sir." Grand Marshal Ratlin just smiled at the notion.

***

Two Nairabian soldiers named Brock and Thomas had just finished their descent down The Mountain of the Three Queens, where a Nairabian brigade waited for them. Thomas was the slenderer of the two and wore a giant, five-inch-tall Mohawk, with the sides of his head being completely shaved to the skin. Thomas carried with him a longbow, in addition to a quiver of arrows as his assigned weapon. Brock, on the other hand, was shorter and stouter than Thomas. He was clearly the more muscular of the two and had shaggy long hair and a moderately full beard as his preferred hairstyle. He was also the hairier of the two, with a considerably excessive amount of body hair. He carried with him two Nairabian scimitars as his weapons. Brock and Thomas were not typical Nairabian warriors. They were part of an elite military scout class with similar skills and abilities as to what you would see from a ranger in a more woodland environment.

Nairabians scouts also always worked in pairs, with one always being a master of archery and the other being a master of duel-wielding scimitars. This was to ensure that they were always ready to defend against both short-ranged and long-ranged attacks when they were out doing their scouting patrols. Additionally, their appearance stood out from a typical Nairabian warrior, because they were also one of the only Nairabian classes to sport leather body armor, as well as be without the classic Nairabian turtle shield.

The majority of the Nairabian brigade that waited for them

at the bottom of the mountain had dispersed into the shadowy areas of the mountainside, doing their best to stay out of the midday heat. Unfortunately for them, there simply wasn't enough mountain shade to accommodate all of them. Many of them were still forced to stand out in the heat of the day, but to take their minds off the heat, many of the soldiers in the unit could be seen conversing with each other, playing cards, snacking on food rations, or participating in any combination of all three.

Brock and Thomas made their way through the scattered soldiers, stopping when they arrived at their brigade commander, General Natalie Wainwright. She was a Nairabian woman with an athletic build of lean muscle and had long brown hair that was secured into a ponytail. She was dressed in scale mail armor, worn over a white tunic, and carried a sheathed bastard sword at her side. Having brown hair wasn't completely unheard of for a Nairabian to have, but it was certainly uncommon.

General Wainwright was accompanied by a Dathen Battle Mage named Denerick Saldore, who was dressed in a hooded, green cloak, with its hood up to protect his head from the sun. However, don't let his pretty cloak fool you, he still had Nairabian blood running through his veins, which meant he was still bigger and stronger than an average Horack Dathen. If Dathen Saldore hadn't had his hood up, you would have seen his undercut hairstyle that had the sides of his head shaved to be almost skintight, while the top of his head was left long and was tied together into a ponytail at the back. He had a thin line of facial hair growth starting at the back of his lower jaw and came together into a slight goatee and mustache. Also, just like General Wainwright, he too wielded a bastard sword and had a shirt of scale mail over his robe to protect him.

Being a part of the elite scout class, Brock and Thomas had

the distinct honor of working directly for the brigade commander.

"What's your report?" General Wainwright asked Brock and Thomas the moment they were within earshot. The two men stopped and immediately rendered a salute to their superior officer.

"Nothing to report, ma'am. Pastoria is just as dull and boring as always," Brock answered her.

"Ma'am," Thomas joined the conversation, "I suggest our plan of action be to make for Sickle Ridge and then hook around to Tenton, that way we can bypass Pastoria unseen. At this rate, we should arrive at Tenton in less than a week."

"Good," General Wainwright answered her two scouts. "Assemble the troops. We're moving out!"

Chapter 5

An Unexpected Meeting

Life as a footman for Enron at Outpost Scorpion was pretty routine. Everyday started off with waking up in the morning and eating breakfast in the dining area, which was an outdoor picnic-like area with several, long wooden tables. Once breakfast was done, it was time for Enron to start his shift guarding the food supplies chamber, located along the outer perimeter of the base. Many of Enron's peers were assigned to duty positions guarding parts of Outpost Scorpion that many would consider to be a bit more worthwhile, like the armory or the headquarters building. Some of the even luckier ones got to leave Outpost Scorpion and go on foot patrols outside the base. But not Enron; he had the unfortunate task of guarding something that he truly believed didn't need to be guarded.

"I mean, who is going to try and steal the food?" Enron would often ask himself, as he drew nonsensical lines in the sand with the edge of his sword. This was awfully childish of Enron to do, but he couldn't help it, he was utterly bored with the seemingly pointless task.

The Horack people had developed the method of storing food in man-made underground chambers. Storing their food underground helped keep the food cooler than it would be if it stayed above ground. Every major town and establishment in the Horack nation had at least one underground storage chamber for food. Enron had known about these storage facilities his entire life, but he had never actually been inside one. Even now, pulling guard duty outside the entrance of one, he still technically hadn't been inside one. All the same, the insides weren't much to look at, given they were usually just full of wooden crates of assorted fruits, vegetables, and cured meats, as well as barrels of water, and sometimes juice. On a super rare occasion, such storage facilities would contain barrels of alcohol as well.

Finally, after five days of being a food guard, Enron got the opportunity he had been waiting for. He was tasked with going on what the more veteran soldiers referred to as a 'Scavenger Mission'. Enron had no idea what to expect from such a mission, but he didn't care either. He was just happy to be leaving the outpost for the first time since he got there.

***

The next morning, Enron and his assigned company marched out of Outpost Scorpion, and out of Pastoria. Despite Enron's excitement for leaving the outpost, he certainly wasn't looking forward to potentially going on another foot march. Fortunately for Enron, upon leaving the gates of Pastoria, he saw a fourteen-vehicle caravan waiting for them. The wagons in the caravan were of a simple wooden, four-wheeled design that were each covered with a canvas material. Each caravan vehicle was completed with two harnessed horses and a driver.

Eight of the wagons had already been filled with occupants by the time Enron and the rest of his company showed up. The eight wagons collectively contained an entire Horack archery company and an entire Horack footmen company. These footmen and archers were the security team that were going as a defensive measure, in case the group was attacked while the others were trying to work. Four of the remaining six wagons were left vacant for Enron and his company to travel in. The last two wagons were also vacant and were left to serve another purpose that Enron wasn't yet aware of.

The caravan departed Pastoria and headed westward towards the border between the Horack and Nairabian nations. The crew traveled for over an hour until the walls of Pastoria disappeared from sight and the open grasslands of Grevanna were all that could be seen.

In order to pass the time on the long journey, Enron tried desperately to strike up a conversation with some of his fellow soldiers. He would ask his companions, "Where are we going?" "What exactly is a 'scavenger mission'?" or even, "What part of Horack are you from?" But it didn't matter, Enron would always get nothing but dead silence as an answer. Enron usually had the pleasure of getting to share billets with people he knew from his time at Warrior Hill, as well as seeing them in passing as he performed his duties, but this wasn't the case for the people in his assigned company. Despite sharing a wagon with nineteen other footmen, none of them were known to him prior to his arrival at Pastoria and none of them wanted anything to do with him. Even as his fellow peers ignored him, Enron noticed that they did not have any trouble still talking amongst themselves. Their conversations mostly consisted of sharing crude and sometimes even sexual jokes and stories with each other.

***

After about two hours of traveling, Enron's caravan came to halt, and his wagon driver immediately turned around and yelled to his passengers, "Alright! This is your stop! Everyone get out!"

The crude conversations that were being had throughout the duration of the ride slowly died down to a dull roar while Enron and the rest of his crew grabbed their gear and disembarked the vehicle. Outside the wagon, Enron, along with everyone else on his team, momentarily squinted at the morning light as their eyes tried to adjust to the sudden brightness change from the inside of their wagon, to the outside sun. The first thing Enron noticed about this new location was the random assortment of weapons, uniforms, and armor that covered the grassy field in front of him. The Horack uniforms were positioned in such a way that they were wrapped in fully fastened leather breastplates. The Horack swords and shields were also placed alongside the uniforms to the left and right. It was almost as if the clothes and equipment did once contain bodies, but had since disappeared, leaving the clothes and equipment where they fell.

A medium-sized mountain ridge also laid to the north of the equipment graveyard. This mountain ridge was known as 'Sickle Ridge', after how its hooked shape resembled a sickle. The sickle-like mountain ridge surrounded the pile of discarded gear in an almost semi-circle like fashion. It also wasn't just Horack weapons and gear that laid discarded and bodiless in the grass, but also giant scimitars and shields belonging to the Nairabians that covered the area as well and were placed in a similar way.

The only thing that seemed normal to Enron about the site was the circle of Horack military officers a short distance away that had accompanied them on their journey. Horack officers were always easy to identify, because they always had a piece of colored, braided, rope wrapped around their right shoulder that decorated their uniforms. The color of the rope also signified the officer's rank: white was for lieutenants, red was for captains, blue was for colonels, and green was for generals. On that day, there weren't any generals present, just six lieutenants, three captains, and one colonel. The lower-ranking officers in the group stood quietly as the colonel spoke to them about the day's mission. Enron recognized Colonel Darrius Calvnar, who stood speaking to the junior officers, but he spoke too quietly for Enron to make out exactly what he was saying to them.

Colonel Calvnar was dressed in a chainmail shirt and wielded a bastard sword. He also had grey hair and a mustache with tips that extended far past his chin and dangled freely below.

"Hey, you're new," Enron suddenly heard a voice behind him.

Enron turned around to see who was speaking to him. It was one of the archers that joined the caravan team as a defensive measure.

"Um, yeah," Enron answered him, not knowing what else to say.

"Hi, I'm Matthew Ester," the archer spoke as he offered his hand to shake.

Enron hesitated for a moment, but then slowly gripped his new acquaintance's hand and gave him a loose-fitted, apprehensive handshake. Enron was pleased that someone finally decided to acknowledge his existence and speak to him.

Enron took advantage of the new potential friend and asked him, "So, what exactly are we doing here? What exactly is a 'scavenger mission' anyway?"

Archer Ester was more than happy to answer his new friend's questions. He said, "One of the unfortunate side effects of the Dathen's post-battle ritual is that any gear or weapons a soldier was carrying at the time of their death is left behind on the battlefield while they get transported from, 'The Dream State, back to Tenton'"

Enron's expression switched to disgust as he looked back at the piles of equipment and clothes on the grassy field before him. He suddenly realized that every single one of those piles of clothes that laid on the battlefield had once contained a dead body that then disappeared from... Enron paused his thoughts for a second and looked back at Ester once more. It had clicked in Enron's head that his new friend had spoken a word that Enron had never heard before.

"Um, Ester? What is 'The Dream State?'" Enron asked.

"Oh, right," Ester answered. "You've never been there, have you?"

Enron slowly shook his head "No."

"Oh, well, um," Ester tried to answer. "Um, don't worry about that right now, you'll find out what it is eventually. Everyone visits 'The Dream State' sooner or later." Ester tried to reassure Enron, but somehow his words were strangely not comforting to him.

Being Enron's first 'scavenger mission', he was afraid of looking like a fool for not knowing what to do, so he had a few more questions for his new friend, Ester. "So, what exactly are we doing here, Ester?" he asked. "What am I expected to do?"

Ester, knowing exactly what it was like being the new guy, was more than happy to inform him. "Well," he started, "I'm a part of the security detail, so my job will be to watch the surrounding area for incoming enemies. However, your job should be to pick up any military gear belonging to the Horack army and place it in the appropriate wagon over there," he explained while pointing to the empty wagons that accompanied them on their trip. "This is how we're able to get uniforms and equipment back into circulation for further use in the army."

Enron prepared to say something in response, but was distracted when the conversation amongst the circle of officers finally ended, and Enron's company commander, Captain Bertock, approached his respective company.

"Alright!" Captain Bertock spoke in a loud, authoritative voice. "This is a standard scavenger mission. Cloth uniforms and armor go in one wagon, shields and weapons go in the other. For the time being, leave all Nairabian weapons and armor where they are. If we have room leftover when we're done, we'll start loading up as much of their equipment as we can afterwards, to be properly disposed of later. For now, focus only on Horack weapons and armor. As always, you are free to keep anything else you find, food or otherwise."

The rest of the soldiers in Enron's company nodded their heads in understanding, for they had done this type of mission many times before. Enron took a moment to look around for reassurance from his new friend Ester, but he had since disappeared from sight. Ester was too busy following his own orders given to him by his commander to march to the top of Sickle Ridge. There, Ester's archery company was to use the high vantage point to survey the surrounding area for any approaching threats.

Enron initially took a moment to observe his fellow footmen, to see how his assigned task was supposed to be done, and then eventually joined them once he had figured it out. There seemed to not be too much of a preferred method for what Horack equipment to focus on first. Some of the soldiers in Enron's company would gather an entire person worth of equipment – uniform, sword, shield, and armor, and carry it all to the wagons to be separated once they got there; while others chose to focus on picking several of the same item, before returning to the wagons with, for example, an armful of swords,

Things seemed to carry on quite peacefully, and possibly even boring for Enron. Although, the same couldn't be said for Ester, who was experiencing a bit more activity from atop Sickle Ridge. One of Ester's fellow archers had spotted a mass of people moving towards them. The mass of people consisted of six marching formations. General Wainwright's brigade had arrived at Sickle Ridge while the Horacks and their far smaller forces were still picking through equipment.

Each Nairabian warrior in General Wainwright's brigade carried with them their iconic turtle shields. Although, at the moment, the turtle shields were still slung over the soldiers' backs, because they were unaware that there were Horack soldiers present on the other side of the ridge. Ester became horrified at the thought of an entire Nairabian brigade of troops marching towards their single Horack battalion. The Horacks were outnumbered two to one!

"What should we do, sir?" Ester asked his commanding officer, Captain Irvine Norvick.

"We should kill them," Captain Norvick spoke, as if the answer was obvious.

"Shouldn't we try to run, sir? We are clearly outnumbered." Ester tried to reason with his commander. However, the suggestion fell on deaf ears.

Captain Norvick turned his head towards his troops and gave the order, "Prepare to fire!"

"But, sir," Ester tried again, but Captain Norvick just waved his hand in the air, metaphorically waving off the attempted notion once more.

On their commander's orders, the archers released a volley of arrows at their longtime enemies, including Ester, who felt at that point he had no other choice. Ester, accepting his fate, sighed deeply and remarked to his peers, "Well, guys, the first round of ghost chicken is on me."

"Only if you get there first!" another archer remarked, upon completing his part in the arrow volley.

The approaching Nairabian soldiers were so completely caught off guard by the incoming arrow attack that they didn't even have time to remove their shields from their backs, much less raise them to protect themselves. Eighty Horack arrows flew and nearly all of them struck, and in some cases, immediately killed a Nairabian soldier. The soldiers of the Nairabian brigade quickly realized they were under attack and swiftly drew out their turtle shell shields and scimitars. The Nairabian archers marching at the back of the brigade also drew out their short sword secondary weapons as well, knowing that their lack of high ground put their bows at a severe disadvantage for the time being. The soldiers that were physically able-bodied enough to do so, then picked up their pace and charged straight for Sickle Ridge.

Captain Norvick quickly ordered another arrow volley, before running to the opposite edge of the mountain, where the rest of the Horack battalion was positioned for their scavenger mission.

"Colonel Calvnar!" he shouted. "We're under attack!"

Colonel Calvnar paused for a second to digest the information and then finally spoke, "Captains! Battle formations! Now!" he ordered his officer subordinates, who were sure to stay in his general vicinity as needed.

Enron's commander, Captain Bertock, immediately fulfilled his superior's bidding by running over to his scattered company, who were still sorting through armor and gear. "Cease operations! Cease operations!" he yelled. "Battle formations!

Now!"

The troops in Enron's company were quick to react to their commander's orders, including Enron himself. Although, the order to get into attack positions did make Enron a bit uneasy. Enron always secretly hoped he would never see the day where he would be expected to participate in open conflict.

In no time at all, Enron and his peers were formed into a single formation with swords drawn and shields raised. Enron's hands coursed with sweat to such an extent that he had a difficult time maintaining his grip on his weapon and shield. While waiting for whatever it was that was coming their way, Enron noticed the remaining infantry companies that had joined them on the caravan trip had created a similarly sized formation to the left of Enron's formation.

The archery company that maintained their firing position atop Sickle Ridge was quickly running out of arrows as they tried to fend off the incoming enemies. With their quivers finally empty, the archery company drew out their short swords and prepared for the inevitable attack. Fortunately for the archers, their role in the battle was temporarily paused. The north side of the ridge was too sheer for the approaching Nairabian army to climb. The only way up was to climb the south side of the mountain. For now, the Nairabian army was forced to move around to the other side of the ridge. The Nairabian army did slow their stride now that the Horack archers had empty quivers and the gauntlet of arrows had ceased.

As the Nairabian brigade rounded the tip of the ridge, the Horack footmen waited on the other side to begin their own charge into battle. Once Colonel Calvnar noticed the archery company had ceased their firing and concluded they had finally run dry on ammunition, he knew it was time to initiate his attack.

Colonel Calvnar and his captains, being the respectable leaders they were, always lead from the front of their formations. Both of the infantry captains had taken their positions centered at the front of their respective companies. Furthermore, centered between the infantry commanders, was Colonel Calvnar himself.

Despite being horribly outnumbered, Enron was the only one present on the battlefield that was clearly afraid. "Wait! Are we really going to do this?" Enron asked anyone who was listening.

A fellow footman next to him smiled and answered, "What are you worried about? You'll be back tomorrow."

"Charge!" Colonel Calvnar ordered with his sword drawn.

Following the order, he and his entire battalion charged into the mass of Nairabians, knowing for certain they were all going to die that day. However, despite their inevitable defeat, many of the Horack soldiers in the battalion smiled and seemed excited for the battle to commence, except for Enron of course.

The battle began as Horack and Nairabian swords clashed. Enron, still not being completely on board with the idea of killing another person, even if it was their enemy, slowed his charge and hesitated.

"Milstrum! Hurry up and kill something!" he heard an adjacent soldier order him.

Enron swallowed hard and accepted what he had to do. He charged into the battle with his longsword drawn, screaming the hardest battle cry he could muster. Then he spotted his first opponent, an average sized Nairabian footman. Enron held his sword high in the air, ready to strike, but it didn't matter; before Enron could even make an attempt to land a hit, he felt a sharp pain to the left of his shoulder. It was the sharpest pain he had ever felt in his life! Enron's sleeveless leather breastplate armor did very little to slow the strike from the massive Nairabian weapon. The Nairabian warrior had quite effortlessly landed a cut in Enron's upper arm. The attack had come in sideways and landed in Enron's deltoid. Enron's body slowly fell backwards, landing on his back. Looking up at the sky, still alive, he saw his opponent enter his field of view once more. Without hesitation, the Nairabian slammed his scimitar into Enron's exposed face, killing him. Enron's eyes closed as everything went black. Enron had ended his first battle without even taking a single person with him. It was a good thing for Enron that every friendly Horack in the battle was too busy trying to keep their own necks intact to have noticed his pathetic death happen.

Chapter 6

The Dream State

Enron remembered the blinding pain in his shoulder that was worse than anything he had ever experienced before. Then, literally in the blink of an eye, it was gone. The next thing Enron remembered was a bright blue light, that slowly turned from blue to blinding white. Slowly, the light faded, and Enron could finally see the world around him once more. Although, it wasn't the world he remembered. Something about this new place told him that he wasn't in Grevanna anymore. Instead, he found himself inside a great hall, the largest great hall Enron had ever been in before, not that he had seen that many in his life up until that point. Enron couldn't see the ends of the hall looking to his left and right, because the great hall was so big that it seemed to be literally endless. Running down the middle of the hall was a long table filled with all sorts of food and things to drink: fire-roasted wild birds, plates of assorted fruit, piles of bread, as well as goblets and mugs of beer, mead, and juice.

"Milstrum! Welcome!" Enron heard a male soldier call out in a surprised, yet pleased, voice.

"Welcome to what?" Enron asked, confused.

"To the brotherhood!" the same male soldier responded, excited.

"Aaaand the sisterhood," another soldier, a female, corrected him.

"And the sisterhood," the same male soldier conceded.

Enron had met these two soldiers before. They were Footman Harth and Footman Kenzi, two of the same people that wouldn't so much as speak a single word to Enron during their trip on the caravan earlier that day. However, they were now greeting him as if they were old friends. Footman Harth had the letters 'D.M.C.' tattooed on his left forearm to represent the initials of his three younger sisters, Danielle, Morgan, and Christina. Footman Harth also had another tattoo on his right pectoral of a Horack round shield with a sword behind it, although it was covered up by his shirt most of the time. Footman Kenzi, on the other hand, had a sleeve-style tattoo of stars in an alternating patterning going down her right arm. Each star was about the size of a small coin.

"So, what is this place?" Enron asked his newly acquired friends.

"This place is most commonly known as 'The Dream State'," Footman Harth, the male soldier, answered him.

"The Dream State? What am I doing here?" Enron asked, still trying to grasp what was going on.

"So, Milstrum," Footman Kenzi began, "I don't know how to tell you this, but you died." Her tone delivering such news wasn't as sorrowful as you may have come to expect from someone delivering the news of someone's death. Instead, her tone was much more matter-of-fact, and almost joking or sarcastic in nature.

"I died?" Enron asked, shocked and confused.

"Yep! But don't feel bad, so did we," Footman Kenzi answered, pointing at herself and Footman Harth next to her.

Enron thought for a moment and then of course easily remembered his foolhardy, yet pathetic death at the hands of a

Nairabian footman.

"So, what are we doing here?" Enron asked after a short pause.

"Waiting," Footman Kenzi answered.

"Waiting for what?" Enron asked.

"For the Dathens to decide to bring us back," Footman Kenzi answered.

Enron felt so stupid for not realizing the obvious answer. He had always known about the Dathen's magical abilities to bring people back from the dead. Although, he never gave much thought to what happened to the deceased soldiers while they waited. Now he knew the answer. By this time, Enron began to notice more of his fellow soldiers appear in the great hall with him, at an increasing tempo. They didn't appear in a puff of smoke, or anything like that. Instead, they faded into the room, starting out relatively transparent and then slowly solidifying. Enron was finally starting to feel comfortable with the new situation, but also noticed that nobody was eating or paying much attention to the food that had been laid out on the massive table.

Enron, who wasn't at all hungry, but wasn't about to give up free food, walked over to the table, grabbed the leg of one of the roasted wild game birds and tore it off. Enron couldn't believe his eyes; the bird's leg immediately replenished itself the second it was detached from the body. Shocked and intrigued, Enron immediately grabbed the regrown leg and tore it from the bird's body. Just like before, it replaced itself right before Enron's eyes again.

"Never-ending food? How wild!" Enron thought to himself, as he now held two roasted bird legs in his hands. Enron smiled and bit deeply into one of the drumsticks he had taken, but his excitement immediately turned to disappointment. What he tasted wasn't food. What he tasted wasn't anything. All he could taste from the poultry leg was air. He couldn't even feel the texture of the food around his mouth. It was as if his mouth went right through it like it wasn't even there.

"We probably should have told you, but you can't eat the food here." Footman Harth laughed.

"You can't eat the food?" Enron asked. "Then what's the point in having it here?"

Footman Harth shrugged his shoulders and said, "I dunno, clearly whoever designed this place didn't think things through very well."

"So, what are we supposed to do here while we wait?" Enron asked, but then, almost as if his words cued the action, he looked to his right, to see a whole roasted bird hurling towards him. Enron instinctively held up his arms in front of his face to block the flying poultry and braced for impact, but the impact never happened. Enron dropped his arms and looked around confused. Apparently, the flying poultry zoomed right through his head as if the bird and his head weren't really there either.

"We mostly just screw around." Footman Harth laughed as he stabbed his assigned longsword straight into Enron's side. However, just like the cooked bird, it went right through him as if the sword and Enron himself weren't really there.

Several minutes passed by as more and more members of Enron's battalion faded into this "Dream State." However, Enron never saw any of the Nairabians from the battlefield come to join him and his Horack buddies, because the Nairabians had their own version of the Dream State they were transported to when they fell in combat. Eventually, even Captain Bertock, Enron's commander showed up to the party, because that's what it was at that point. Everywhere you looked, soldiers were pretending to fight with their assigned weapons and throwing food and drinks at each other. Even Captain Bertock, a man that Enron had always pictured as being a serious, no-nonsense kind of person, joined in on the shenanigans.

Archer Ester and the rest of his archery company were some of the last ones to fall during the battle that was still taking place at Sickle Ridge. But just like everyone else in the battalion, Ester did eventually join his friends in the Dream State.

"Ester? What are you doing here?" Enron asked him as soon as he saw his friend fade in. However, Enron quickly realized the stupidity of asking a question with such an obvious answer.

Archer Ester smiled and mentally waved off the question. It wasn't the first time he had been asked that question in this place. Ester sarcastically spoke, "Oh, you know, the view from the ridge was getting a bit stale, so I thought I would join you guys here."

Both Enron and Ester snickered at the remark. Then, after a short and some-what awkward silence, Ester spoke again, "It's probably to no surprise, but we lost the fight, Enron."

"What?" Enron replied, not knowing what else to say.

"Don't act so surprised, Enron. It's not like we even had a chance," Ester spoke. "Besides," Ester continued, "it's not like winning this particular battle would have won the war for us anyways. It's just another fight in this endless war. And best of all, we all get to go home after this."

Enron nodded in understanding. He and Ester continued to enjoy the party of fallen soldiers with the rest of the members of their battalion. A common point of discussion during the party was asking each other how many enemies everyone had managed to kill before they were killed themselves.

Enron would always lie whenever he was asked the question and make up a number by saying, "Oh, you know, like two or three, I think."

Saying that he had taken two or three Nairabians with him seemed like a reasonable number for someone's very first battle. Besides, any number was still better than his actual kill count, zero.

Enron spent the remainder of his time hanging out with Ester; that was, until Ester began to slowly disappear right before Enron's eyes. Ester had been sharing a story with Enron at the time, but literally stopped mid-sentence and disappeared from sight.

Enron, confused by the new event, turned to Footman Harth, who had been standing with them at the time, and asked him, "What's going on with him?"

"He's going back home," Footman Harth answered. "The Dathens at Tenton have discovered that they have people here that need to be brought back, so they have begun their ritual. He's being resurrected, and soon you and I will join him."

Enron broke eye contact from Footman Harth to look back at Archer Ester, but he was already gone. Enron then looked back at Footman Harth to say something, but found that he couldn't. Enron opened his mouth to speak, but no words would come out. Enron could also tell that Footman Harth was trying to tell him something, but just like Enron's words that refused to be spoken, Footman Harth's words refused to be heard, at least by Enron. Footman Harth then started to go blurry, and a bright blue light, similar to the one that had brought Enron to this state, showed up again and was again followed by the same bright white light. Then, the bright white light slowly faded to black.

Through the blackness, Enron heard a familiar voice speak, "Welcome home, son."

Chapter 7

Returning Home

Enron woke up in a room made of stone, that was illuminated by an unseen source that seemed to emanate from everywhere at once. Enron could also feel the coldness of stone on his bare back. The literally stone-cold object he laid on made him realize something. For reasons Enron didn't yet understand, he was completely naked. Enron looked up to see his father, Dathen Guardian Mortagart Milstrum, standing over him.

"Dad? Where am I? And where are my clothes?" Enron exclaimed.

"No time to explain, son, I need you to get off the table so I can get ready for the next person to be brought back. For now, please just follow Sarah into the next room," Dathen Milstrum answered, while motioning his hand towards a woman dressed in white, holding a folded-up robe in her hands.

Enron's gaze shifted from looking at his father to looking at 'Sarah' standing in the corner, confirming there was indeed a woman in the room with him. Enron, embarrassed, immediately covered his exposed privates with his hands to hide them. Enron then felt his father's hand on his bare shoulder begin to pull him off the stone table.

"Come on, son, I need you to move so I can get ready for the next person," Dathen Milstrum ordered his son.

Enron, trusting his father, as well as not wanting to disobey one of his parents, did as he was told. Dathen Milstrum pushed his son in the direction of the woman in the corner once he was properly on his feet. Enron, still doing his best to cover himself, slowly inched over to the waiting woman. On his way over to her, Enron noticed eight upright barrels that had their lids removed, revealing their contents, and he could clearly see they were filled with some kind of sand. Enron couldn't be sure of it, but he assumed that the barrels were filled with the magic sand he knew his father needed to perform Dathen spells.

Enron, with his head lowered, spoke to the woman. "Sarah, um, I'm sorry for, um, for my appearance, ma'am."

Sarah laughed, "Please! Do you really think you're the first man I've ever seen naked? I see people like you almost every day!"

Enron didn't like the idea that his nakedness was seen as a joke to the woman, but he did feel better that his appearance wasn't seen as being offensive to her.

"First time in this room, huh?" Sarah asked Enron rhetorically. She then handed Enron the folded-up garment she held in her hands and said, "Here! Put this on. This should make you feel better."

Enron immediately snatched the folded robe from her hands and dressed himself with it in the blink of an eye. Once dressed, Sarah lead Enron into the next room, which contained many wooden tables set up in rows, with numerous piles of folded clothes on them. Enron immediately recognized the piles of clothes as Horack military uniforms. There was also a stone spiral staircase in the back corner of the room.

"Milstrum, Milstrum," Sarah began speaking Enron's last name, while lightly digging through the piles of clothes. "Ah-ha!" she spoke again, after finding the pile of clothes she had been looking for. "E. Milstrum," she continued to speak, as she picked up and handed Enron the stack of uniforms.

"Alright, Milstrum, you see that staircase back there?" Sarah asked.

Enron looked in the direction Sarah was pointing and saw the stone staircase she was talking about.

Unfortunately, Sarah didn't give Enron enough time to give a response before she carried on with her instructions. "Take your clothes, head upstairs, and get dressed in the changing room up there. Then hurry up and exit the room before the next soldier comes back, or you will find yourself getting dressed with a friend." She laughed. "And then finally, and most importantly, make sure you head immediately to Tenton Keep and get refitted for gear. From there, you can either stay in the spare Tenton Keep barracks while you wait for your orders to return to your duty assignment, or, since you have family here, you can stay with your family if you wish. The choice is up to you."

Enron scaled the staircase as instructed, while awkwardly holding his white robe closed as he went. He entered a square room that was lined with more smokeless torches like he had seen before. He began to unfold the clothes he had been given and almost immediately noticed that both the uniform pants and shirt were embroidered with "E. Milstrum," on the tags like the two other copies of his uniform he had been issued before, at Tenton Keep. Enron finished getting dressed and walked through the only door in the room he could find, assuming this had to be the exit Sarah was talking about.

Enron was immediately met with bright, mid-day sunlight upon leaving the room, because he was clearly outside, but more importantly, he was standing outside The Temple in Tenton. Enron looked around, amazed at where he had just come from.

He had never been allowed inside The Temple before, and now he was leaving it for the first time in his life! he also had no idea The Temple had underground chambers, because he always thought it just consisted of the three small buildings on the ground floor.

Enron looked to his left and then to his right, completely forgetting most of the information Sarah had just given him. However, he did remember something about "since you have family here, you can stay your with family if you wish," so without hesitation, Enron turned right and headed in the direction of his home, but you could say it wasn't *his* home anymore. Officially speaking, his home was still back in Pastoria, in the barracks he had been assigned to.

Enron sprinted as fast as he could, nearly knocking a couple of people over as he went, but he didn't care, he was just happy he going to his parents' home. Unfortunately, his happiness soon turned to disappointment when he entered the home to discover that it was completely vacant. Enron wasn't expecting his father or brother to be there, he knew where they were. His father was of course still at The Temple performing rituals and his brother had been reassigned elsewhere. However, he was at least expecting his mother and sister to be home, but they weren't. Enron walked into his old room in a last-ditch effort to locate his family, but just like before, it was empty.

Just as Enron was getting ready to leave his old room, he caught his reflection in a floor mirror. It was the same floor mirror that Enron used to admire his military uniform and gear just over a month ago. He took a hard look at his face to see that it showed absolutely no signs of damage from being struck by the Nairabian that killed him. He felt his face to see if he could feel any kind of markings or scars that hadn't been there before, but Enron felt nothing out of the ordinary. Enron then directed his attention to his left shoulder. Taken over by curiosity, he removed his uniform linen shirt to expose his left shoulder. It too was completely free of any signs of injury from the battle. Enron had always known about the Dathens' ability to bring back the dead after falling in combat. After all, Enron's own father was a Dathen Guardian and his older brother, Jonas, had been a soldier in the war for the past several years and had died and been brought back countless times. However, getting to experience the phenomenon firsthand still felt very foreign to him.

Enron put his shirt back on and finally exited the room. Back in the main room of his old home, Enron sighed deeply, not really sure what to do with himself. Enron spotted a large chest next to him that he knew very well. It was his family's dry food storage box. Enron flipped the lid of the chest open and looked inside for a snack. The chest was well organized with flatbreads neatly stacked against one of the corners of the box. Assorted fruits were also piled together according to type, among other foods. Enron looked for the cured meats for the potential source of his snack, but there were only a few scraps of meat left and he didn't want to seem greedy, so he grabbed an apple instead. Enron was munching on the apple with his back to the main entrance of the room, when he felt someone come up from behind him and give him a hug.

It was his mother, Dillia. "Welcome home, son," she spoke softly, releasing him from her embrace.

"How did you know I was coming home?" he asked her.

"I didn't," she answered. "It's just that nothing surprises me anymore."

Enron examined his mother's face. She was smiling the same smile she always did whenever she was happy to see him, but for some reason, Enron was expecting more from her. Her eyes weren't tearing up with joy, she was just smiling normally – that's all.

"I thought she would be happier to see me," Enron thought to himself, "Doesn't she know I was dead for several hours?"

Unknown to Enron, he had actually been dead for closer to several days than the several hours he had assumed, but this wasn't Enron's fault. He wasn't aware that time passed at a slower rate in The Dream State than it did in the real world. A single hour in The Dream State took about as long to pass as an entire day did in the real world.

But it was just like Enron's mother had said before, nothing surprised her anymore. After all, Enron wasn't her first son to die in combat and come back again. She had gotten so used to it with Jonas that there was no need to express any level of concern when the same thing happened to her youngest son as well.

Enron and his mother spent the next couple of hours talking about life at his assignment in Pastoria. Although, it was pretty difficult for him to make guarding a storage locker with the scent of manure hanging in the air sound interesting. Eventually, Mika came home from visiting a friend.

"Enron!" Mika exclaimed the moment she walked into the house. She then immediately ran up to Enron and gave him the biggest, tightest hug she had ever given him.

"Um, hi, Mika. Miss me much?" Enron asked his sister.

"What?" she asked. "I'm not allowed to be happy to see my brother?"

Enron rolled his eyes. She had a point. Also, if Enron's memory served, she acted the exact same way the first couple of times Jonas returned from the Dream State, but it eventually subsided.

"So, big brother, how many people have you killed?" Mika asked Enron. "OW!" she then exclaimed after her mother whacked her on the shoulder for the inappropriate question. Enron's mother then shook her head in a chastising manner at her young daughter.

"Come, Mika," Dillia called to her daughter. "Come help me make dinner." Dillia then smiled at Enron and spoke again, "You're welcome to join us too, Enron."

Together, Dillia and Mika made a meal of honey-roasted carrots and cornbread, with enough to feed four people: Dillia, Mika, Enron, and Enron's father, Mortagart. However, Dathen Milstrum didn't show up for dinner that night.

Dillia sighed. "Your father must be working late tonight, keeping up with the rituals," she spoke to her children.

Enron's father did eventually make it home a couple of hours later, but he had a look that was a mix of exhaustion and sadness on his face.

"We lost Dathen Lord Gabriel Benedict tonight," he spoke very somberly, clearly holding back tears.

Chapter 8

Guests at the Milstrum House

Dillia escorted her husband by the arm, over to their dining table.

"Well," Mortagart spoke, forcing a smile, "here's some good news, Enron. It looks like you'll be staying with us for a couple of more days than originally planned."

"What?" Enron asked, confused.

"Yeah," Mortagart answered. "The council has ordered that all outgoing troop movements out of Tenton be temporarily ceased. The council wants maximum participation for Dathen Benedict's funeral, which is scheduled to take place in three days."

On the outside, Enron nodded somberly in the face of the sorrowful moment, but on the inside, he was smiling. He was happy that he was going to get to spend three days relaxing with his family. He was also happy to not have to deal with the military life for a while.

***

Enron woke up the next morning in a mild panic. He had finally remembered the additional information Sarah had given him the day before. The vital information about not forgetting to go immediately to Tenton Keep, to be refitted for gear after he was finished getting dressed. Enron put on his uniform and sprinted to Tenton Keep, the whole time fearing what may happen to him for showing up to get gear a day late. Were they going to deny him gear? Were they going to make fun of him for forgetting? In reality, what happened was: nothing, absolutely nothing. The gear and supply clerks at Tenton Keep were so used to handing out gear to soldiers every day that they had no way of knowing if Enron was a part of the surge of troops that came in the day before, or if he was separate from them and was requesting gear for other reasons. It turned out that Enron was panicked about the whole situation for no reason at all.

Also, on an even brighter note, this time Enron was issued a replacement longsword and round shield that seemed to be in a better condition than the first set he had been issued prior to going to Pastoria. The sword and shield still had markings of obvious use all over it, but both items seemed to lack any signs of major repairs. His new round shield certainly wasn't missing a large chunk from its outer rim that had been haphazardly replaced with a scrap piece of wood, like the last one.

Then a thought entered Enron's mind, "Where is my original sword and shield?" He imagined they were still on the ground somewhere by Sickle Ridge where he had dropped them after being slain by the Nairabian enemy. Enron was of course absolutely right. That was exactly where his equipment had been left. The Horacks had a great system in play that allowed them to recycle gear that had been used by a fallen soldier. Once a battle was complete, providing Horack soldiers were able to get to the area first, they would conduct a scavenger mission for any dropped equipment that was still in a usable condition. The equipment would be collected up just like Enron had done before, and it would be sent off to all the supply depots across the Horack nation, to supply the Horack troops as needed. That also explained why Enron's first shield showed such heavy signs of damage and why even his new shield, which was in better condition than his last, still shows signs of moderate use.

***

The next day, things began to pick up for the Milstrum family. That morning, they enjoyed a breakfast of toasted bread, topped with some kind of fruit spread.

Suddenly, a man dressed in a Dathen Battle Mage's uniform, announced himself from outside the Milstrum residence. "Dathen Battle Mage Lucas Chaims here to see Dathen Guardian Milstrum."

Mortagart's ears immediately perked up at the announcement. Excited, Mortagart stood up to greet the Milstrum family's new guest. In walked Dathen Chaims, a younger-looking man in his early thirties. Dathen Chaims, escorted by Mortagart, walked two more steps forward into their home, before everyone in the room heard Dillia Milstrum forcibly clear her throat.

Mortagart winced for a second and stated. "Oh, right. I'm sorry, old friend, but the missus has a strict policy of 'no weapons in the house.'"

Dathen Chaims smiled and nodded. He wasn't married himself, but he could understand Mortagart Milstrum wanting to do whatever he needed to do to please his wife. Dathen Chaims immediately removed his belt containing his sword, neatly wrapped itself around the sheath bit of the sword, and set it on the floor by the room's entrance. However, Dathen Chaims kept his chainmail shirt on, because it wasn't technically a weapon.

"You got here pretty quickly, brother," Mortagart spoke to

his colleague, "for someone who traveled here all the way from Outpost Waynard."

'Outpost Waynard' was a Horack base off the shores of Peace River and was the nearest Horack establishment to the Nairabian border.

"Don't forget, old friend, I have 'Milky' to help carry me on the journey from Waynard," Dathen Chaims answered Mortagart.

Just then, everyone in the room heard 'Milky', a horse with a black and white spotted pattern resembling that of a stereotypical cow, snort from outside the home.

Every single Horack Dathen was taught how to ride a horse as a part of their Dathen training. This was to give them the ability to easily travel from one location to another as needed, without having to take a marching party like Enron had to take to Pastoria. Even Dathen Guardian Milstrum knew how to ride a horse, but he very seldom did anymore, seeing as he had no real need to leave Tenton for any reason, like he used to when he was still a Battle Mage.

"I rode straight through the night as soon as I heard about Dathen Lord Benedict's passing," Dathen Chaims continued.

Dathen Chaims and Dathen Milstrum, along with the rest of the Milstrum family present in Tenton that day, continued to chat and catch up on lost time for several more moments, all while each enjoying a cup of tea, except for Mika, who wasn't a big fan of tea and opted to have a cup of juice instead. Once all the tea had been finished and the juice had been drunk, Dathen Chaims dismissed himself from the conversation as well as the Milstrum house to give himself time to find his own accommodations for the next few days, while he prepared and waited for the funeral happening later on that week.

Dillia had barely finished cleaning up breakfast before

another guest announced themselves to the Milstrum house, in a similar fashion as Dathen Chaims had done earlier. It was Nicolas Dunheimer, a twenty-four-year-old man who, due to Dathen Lord Benedict's passing, had graduated from being Dathen Apprentice Dunheimer, to Dathen Battle Mage Dunheimer.

Once again, it was Mortagart Milstrum who answered the door. "Ah, Welcome *Dathen Battle Mage* Dunheimer," Mortagart greeted their newest guest, sounding legitimately happy for the newest official member to his team.

Although, as much as Dathen Milstrum was happy for Dathen Battle Mage Dunheimer, Dathen Dunheimer couldn't be happier, for he was beaming with pride and strutting around like he was the hottest thing to come to Tenton that day.

Enron was never too fond of the newly promoted Dathen. Enron and Dathen Dunheimer had known each other since Dathen Dunheimer was ten and Enron was four. Growing up, Dathen Dunheimer was always in the Milstrum home, training with Enron's father on how to be a Dathen, occasionally even spending the night there on a collapsible cot, borrowed from The Temple. Dathen Dunheimer had become like the brother Enron never wanted.

At twenty-four years old, Dathen Dunheimer wasn't the oldest Dathen Apprentice in Horack history, but he was definitely one of them. Due to the nature of the Dathen promotion system, it was possible for a Dathen Apprentice to be just about any age prior to them making their transition to Dathen Battle Mage. In Horack history, the oldest Dathen Apprentice to ever exist went to Jacqueline Mundar, who was twenty-eight when she graduated to Dathen Battle Mage. Also, the record for the youngest Dathen Battle Mage goes to Robbie Mason, who was fourteen at the time of joining the ranks with the rest of his Dathen team. It was also the nature of the Dathen promotion system that a Dathen Apprentice to not see any sort of combat prior to their Battle Mage promotion. Despite Enron's non-exist kill count from his first battle, Enron technically had more combat experience than the twenty-four-year-old who stood before him.

Having one guest be immediately followed by another was to be expected for the Milstrum family, considering the situation. The three Dathens that resided outside of Tenton were all making their way to the city to attend the funeral of their beloved Dathen Lord leader. However, each Dathen subordinate was almost required to stop by Dathen Milstrum's house, because he was still seen as their superior. Dathen Jasmine Blanes, the only female Horack Dathen at the time and the newest Dathen Guardian next to Dathen Milstrum, was sure to pay her visit to Mortagart early the next day. Dathen Guardian Blanes was a slender female with the same deep black hair that was common to the Horack people. Her hair was tied together into a neat side braid that came down the front of her right shoulder. Finally, Hector Vangoff, the Dathen Battle Mage who managed to melt half the face off a Nairabian warrior during the defense of Rogue's Mountain Keep, showed up late on the second night.

The only living member of the Dathen crew that hadn't paid Mortagart a visit was Dathen Guardian George Grook, who was soon to be Dathen Lord George Grook. Dathen Grook was still Mortagart's superior and it was up to Mortagart to pay him a visit, not the other way around. Mortagart approached the two-room home of Dathen Grook in the early evening of the second day, prior to Dathen Vangoff's visit to Tenton. Dathen Grook, being a childless widower, didn't have any need for a larger, full-sized residence like the Milstrum family.

"Dathen Guardian Mortagart Milstrum, here to see Dathen

Lord George Grook," Mortagart announced, as if he needed to specify who he was there to see, seeing as Dathen Grook lived alone.

"Enter, Milstrum," Dathen Grook granted him.

Dathen Grook and Dathen Milstrum could both loosely be considered friends, but at the same time, Dathen Grook hated being on a first name basis with just about anyone. Dathen Milstrum entered the very dimly lit room. The only light sources present was what little light was coming in through the windows from the setting sun, as well as light coming from half a dozen lit candles surrounding the urn of Dathen Grook's deceased wife, that was placed on an adjacent table against the wall. Dathen Grook was sitting in a chair with a gray tunic on.

"So, big day tomorrow, George," Dathen Milstrum spoke.

Dathen Grook nodded gently. The two sat in mildly awkward silence for a moment, because Dathen Milstrum didn't really know what else to say. He knew that George was going to be officially switching from 'Dathen Guardian' to 'Dathen Lord' the next day and therefore he knew he had to have a lot on his mind. Although, it was Dathen Grook who broke the silence.

"We're going to have to find a new apprentice soon, Milstrum."

"Uh, yeah!" Dathen Milstrum spoke, relieved that Dathen Grook was talking.

"So, uh, um," Dathen Milstrum searched his brain for a good candidate for the job. Finally, his first suggestion came to him. "Uh! There's a boy my wife, Dillia, teaches at the school. From what I hear, I think he would be worth looking into. Um, Anthony, I think his name is."

"I don't know this 'Anthony', but we can look into him," Dathen Grook spoke. "I also think Mika would also be a good candidate worth looking into."

"Mika? My daughter, Mika?" Dathen Milstrum spoke with a disturbed tone in his voice. "Absolutely not!"

"Look, your daughter is smart and is a quick learner. You should be honored I would suggest her. Besides, you already have two sons fighting on the front lines of this war, why is she so different?" Dathen Grook asked.

"The difference is that she is my daughter!" Dathen Milstrum proclaimed.

Dathen Grook just grinned at his colleague's lame excuse. Dathen Milstrum stormed out of Dathen Grook's home, angry. Dathen Grook had never seen Dathen Milstrum angry in all the years he had worked with him, but clearly Dathen Grook's suggestion to make his daughter, Mika Milstrum, a Dathen had touched a nerve.

Chapter 9

Funeral

On the morning of the funeral, everyone in Tenton who was able to show up was in attendance to pay the deceased Dathen Lord their respects. More than ten thousand people crowded around the courtyard area of The Temple, and spilled far into the streets. Most of those who were attending the funeral had a difficult time seeing what was going on during the mostly standing room only event. The only seats present at the funeral were located at the front of the ceremony and were filled by the newly promoted Dathen crew, the thirty Horack council members, and about a dozen other chairs for close friends and family of the recently deceased, and other dignitaries.

Two of the dignitaries included in the limited seating were Grand Marshal Baker and his assistant, Deputy Grand Marshal Stalls. Grand Marshal Alexander Baker was the commander of the entire Horack army. He was an older man with white hair that was trimmed into a buzz cut. His most defining feature was that he was missing his right leg. Grand Marshal Baker had lost his leg when it was severed in combat during his last battle, about five years ago. A Nairabian Dathen Battle Mage had used an Acid Spell that melted away most of the Grand Marshal's leg, but it also managed to cauterize the wound as well. The cauterized wound saved the Grand Marshal's life, but left him permanently without a leg. Now all that was left of his right leg was a wooden prosthetic. Because he didn't technically die, he wasn't able to be brought back with the Resurrection Spell and therefore, his leg remained permanently gone.

Many non-Dathens had made the suggestion of intentionally killing the Grand Marshal for the sole purpose of bringing him back from the Dream State, with his leg fully intact again. However, doing so would be considered to be breaking Dathen Law. Dathen Law stated that you can only use the Resurrection Spell to bring back those who died in combat. Intentionally killing the Grand Marshal would be seen more as a murder than it would be a combat casualty. Grand Marshal Baker was just another one of the few ex-soldiers unfortunate enough to fall into this technicality.

It was understood that not having the ability to properly fight in combat had put limitations on someone so skilled as he, but given his extensive experience, knowledge, and military expertise, he was able to spend the last years of his career as a military thinker and decision maker, until he was eventually promoted to Grand Marshal. Grand Marshal Baker's assistant, Deputy Grand Marshal Dexter Stalls sat to his right. He was a scrawny individual who perpetually looked hungry. He wore a pair of spectacles that were constantly sliding down his narrow nose. Lacking the muscle mass of even your typical Horack soldier, Deputy Grand Marshal Stalls was never very useful on the battlefield. However, with his superior intelligence, as well as his father being one of the thirty council members, he was able to easily secure the prestigious position next to Grand Marshal Baker. Also, Deputy Grand Marshal Stall's ability to think with logic that was completely free of emotion made him a perfect chief advisor to the Grand Marshal.

One hundred armed Horack soldiers stood off to the side in

two formations of fifty as a way to show the Horack military presence. Enron, however, wasn't one of the soldiers in the formation. He wasn't technically assigned to Tenton as a soldier, so he was free to watch the ceremony from the sidelines with his mother and sister. He, like his Tenton counterparts, was dressed in his military uniform, however, unlike his Tenton counterparts, he was unarmed. It was so crowded that carrying a weapon would have been seen as an unnecessary poking hazard. Despite the relatively unarmed soldier presence at the ceremony, the town wasn't completely defenseless. The regular Horack soldiers assigned to the security detachment still maintained their regular positions along the Tenton outer wall and defense towers.

The deceased Dathen Lord Gabriel Benedict laid in a wooded casket of oak, which was placed on top of a pyre in preparation for his cremation. Tenton, being as big as it was, simply didn't have a realistic amount of room for a proper cemetery. That's why it was mandatory to be cremated whenever anyone died of non-combat related causes in Tenton. Other civilizations in Horack that laid outside of Tenton were, in some cases, given the option to have a cemetery on site. A prime example would be Pastoria. Those who died of non-combat related causes in those areas were then given the option to be buried or cremated. Unfortunately, those who lived in Tenton were not given that option.

***

Each Dathen present gave their own heartfelt eulogy, starting with Dathen Guardian Milstrum, moving down the chain to the newly appointed Dathen Guardian Jasmine Blanes. The series of eulogies continued through each of the Dathen Battle Mages and was finished off by the crew's newest Dathen Battle Mage, Nicolas Dunheimer, followed by the new Dathen Lord George Grook. This pattern was picked to ensure the newest Dathen member wasn't put on the spot by going first, but also ensuring the Dathen with the highest position was the last one to speak.

Each Dathen then took a lit torch from ground stakes that were specifically designed to hold torches. Each torch was lit naturally with the use of flint and steel, instead of the magically created Dathen way of using a simple spell to make smokeless fire torches. Each Dathen evenly surrounded their deceased leader and simultaneously set fire to the pyre. With eyes welling up with tears, everyone within eyesight of the prestigious dignitary momentarily watched the flames grow around the woodpile. However, their meditative stares were quickly interrupted by a bell sounding far off in the distance. A warning bell…

Chapter 10

Attack on Tenton

Archer Eric Menderson pulled on the long rope, which was attached to the bell at the top of his assigned bell tower, with all his strength. Tenton was under attack, and Archer Menderson was forced to complete a task he hoped he would never have do during his military career: ring the warning bell.

"Menderson! Cease that ring!" Sergeant Bullrum ordered Archer Menderson. "You've rung that dang thing so many times that even the dead have heard you!"

With his triceps throbbing, Archer Menderson nodded to his superior. Archer Menderson looked out over the horizon from his position on top of the Tenton outer defense wall to see the Nairabian army quickly approaching from the northwest. The entire Nairabian army that was present had spent many nights on a far-from-view plateau, waiting for their time to attack, and their time was now. Archer Menderson quickly readied an arrow, like his archery peers had already done, in preparation for the approaching battle. His hand trembled while holding his bowstring, partially from the muscle exhaustion in his arms and partially from nervousness. Archer Menderson was still a new soldier in the Horack army, and he had never seen combat up until that point.

The two brigades of Nairabian footmen marched with their shields raised in their classic Testudo formation. The only other

Nairabians on site at the time were in the Nairabian archery brigade that was behind the two footmen brigades, and was out of range of Horack attacks. As always, most of the Horack arrows bounced off the raised shields of the Nairabian footmen harmlessly. The Horacks tasked with defending Tenton were left without the aid of catapults to break the Nairabian shields, like there was at the battle of Rogue's Mountain Keep. Although, they did have light ballista teams as their form of heavy artillery.

Unfortunately, those inadequate weapons didn't do much to slow the Nairabian advance. Over sixty-five percent of the ballista bolts bounced harmlessly off the advancing horde like their weaker arrow counterparts. However, the handful of ballista bolts that still pierced the Nairabian's abnormally hard shields was still better than nothing, so the Horacks still continued to fire their ballista artillery as quickly as they could crank them out. Up until that point, the Nairabians had never been brave enough to attack the Horack capital and therefore, the Horacks had overlooked upgrading its defenses to catapults like they had done at so many other defensible positions around their nation.

The three brigades of Nairabian troops came to a halt about a hundred feet from the Tenton defense wall. Although, the halted formation didn't do much to stop the continued barrage of ballista bolts raining down on them. After a very short pause, two members from two of the brigades present, dropped their raised shields, seemingly exposing themselves to enemy attack. The two men were dressed in dark green robes and scale mail shirts, for they were both Nairabian Dathen Battle Mages. One of the Dathen Battle Mages stood completely unafraid as a Horack arrow hurled itself towards him. The arrow stopped literally inches from the exposed Dathen's face and immediately exploded into a hundred splinters, as if the Dathen was being protected by some unseen force. In fact, he was. Both of these Nairabian Dathen Battle Mages had casted Armor Spells on themselves prior to the battle. This was done as a precaution to protect them while they prepared for their next part of their mission. This spell also made the Nairabian turtle shields the two Dathens carried with them seem like a bit of a redundancy, but it was necessary to help them blend in with the rest of the Testudo Formation.

The two Dathens, placing their mission above the lives and safety of those in front of them, began pushing soldiers out of their way to take up new positions at the front of the formation. Upon reaching the fronts of their respective brigades, both Battle Mages reached into their bags of magic sand and begin preparing for another spell. With magic sand in hand, they both started speaking the necessary incantation for the spell, almost in unison, for they were both preparing to cast the same spell. Both handfuls of sand began to glow blue as they approached completion of the incantation. When the spell was complete, they both threw their glowing blue sand balls at the stone wall that surrounded the perimeter of Tenton. Both of the blue sand balls immediately exploded on contact with the wall, together blasting a huge hole in it. The ground shook violently as soldiers on top of the wall were thrown off. Many of the soldiers were killed instantly from the shockwave of the blast, while some were killed upon impact from hitting the ground below, and still others were killed from flying debris. Archer Menderson was one of the unfortunate people caught in the blast. The young archer died almost instantly and was well on his way to visiting The Dream State for his very first time.

***

As soon as everyone who was attending Dathen Lord Benedict's funeral heard the loud blast coming from the edge of town, their expressions turned from suspicious curiosity that the warning bell had been a false alarm, to confirmed panic that Tenton was truly under attack. The two platoon sergeants in charge of the two armed platoons present at the funeral both immediately ordered their soldiers to break formation and to run in the direction of the loud explosion everyone had just heard.

The two platoons weren't even out of sight when Dathen Lord George Grook stood up on his chair. "Alright, Vangoff, Chaims, Dunheimer," he began to announce, but stopped mid-sentence, realizing it was far too loud for anyone to hear him. Everyone who was still present at the funeral was too busy panicking and making a commotion, due to the apparent attack that was occurring.

"SILENCE!" Dathen Lord Grook shouted. The commotion then slowly began to die down on his order. "Now," he began again. "Vangoff, Chaims, and Dunheimer, go assist as needed at the wall. Vangoff, you're in charge."

The three Horack Battle Mages nodded their heads and immediately ran off in the direction of the wall, as ordered.

"Blanes, Milstrum," he continued, before giving a deep sigh. "You're staying with me. You're going to be my protection." It pained Dathen Lord Grook to admit it, but he had to realize how important his life was now and that he required protection.

Dathen Lord Grook recomposed himself and continued once more. "To all of the other soldiers present, you need to head to the armory and arm yourselves." Dathen Lord Grook then took a moment to look at the crowd of people. He was looking for a particular person in the crowd. "Anthony Jenkins! Where are you?" Dathen Grook shouted to the crowd.

"HERE!" Anthony Jenkins shouted, with his hand raised. Anthony Jenkins was a fifty-seven-year-old war veteran who left his war days behind him twelve years prior, when he reached the soldier retirement age of forty-five. For the past twelve years, he had been leading and designing a militia force in Tenton as a precaution, in case Tenton ever became under attack, like it was now. Anthony Jenkins was, of course, an older-looking man with tired eyes and with greyish-white hair that came together into a messy, masculine-style ponytail.

"Anthony Jenkins," Dathen Grook continued. "I leave the decisions of your militia up to you. Everyone else who isn't in the town militia, should go to their homes and hide. Also, grab anything you can use as a weapon to protect yourselves as needed."

Everyone present who was listening to Dathen Lord Grook immediately followed his orders upon hearing the particular order that pertained to them. The soldiers and of course the other Dathens had no problems hearing what Dathen Lord Grook had to say, and fortunately, a good portion of the civilian population were able to hear their new Dathen Lord's orders. The civilians that were too far away to hear him had the messages conveyed to them by other passing civilians on their way to their homes, as instructed.

***

A good number of Nairabian warriors had managed to enter the city through the hole that had been blasted into the wall by their two Dathens, by the time the one hundred Horack soldiers from the ceremony and the two reserve Horack brigades stationed at

Tenton Keep had arrived at the wall. The two reserve brigades had heard the warning bell, just as the funeral goers had, and quickly made haste to the wall to defend it. Unfortunately for the Horacks and their two-plus brigade-sized force, they were still considered to be outnumbered by their three Nairabian brigade opponents. Having no choice but to accept their odds and fight, one of the Horack brigades charged at the Nairabian's left flank, while the other brigade wheeled around to the Nairabian's front. The remaining one hundred ceremony soldiers quickly mobbed up with the brigade leading the frontal attack.

A few minutes later the Dathen Battle Mages, lead by Dathen Vangoff, reached the battle as well. Surveying the area, Dathen Vangoff put his arm out to stop his two teammates, because at that moment he had managed to come up with a battle plan for him and his team to execute. Dathen Vangoff led his team around to the back of the two reserve brigades leading the attack, making sure to avoid as much of the conflict as they could – for now. Safely shielded by their Horack teammates, Dathen Vangoff and his people continued their movements to the Tenton defense wall and followed the wall until they came to one of the ladders that led to yet another one of the warning bell towers.

The three Dathens went up the warning bell tower ladder and onto the top of the wall. There, they were immediately met with a number of Horack archers who had been doing their best to fend off the Nairabians outside the wall that were still funneling into the city. The Dathen Battle Mage crew lead by Dathen Vangoff pushed through the archers that were crowding the walkways on the wall. The crew continued under an archway that held a ballista firing team above it, until they found the perfect spot to execute Dathen Vangoff's plan. Dathen Vangoff halted his men and gave the order, "Alright, let's blast 'em!"

The Dathen Battle Mages immediately readied the same Dathen spell their Nairabian counterparts had used to blast a hole in the Tenton defense wall earlier. BOOM, BOOM, BOOM! The three magically created explosions went off, each leaving a crater, as well as dead Nairabian footmen in their wake. The Blast Spells were effective enough at killing their Nairabian enemies, but the Dathen Battle Mages still had to act quickly, for they could only safely kill the Nairabian invaders while they were still outside their city. Once they were within the city walls, the Dathen Battle Mages ran the risk of killing their own people caught within the radius of their Blast Spells. Dathen Vangoff and his crew each launched another round of Blast Spell attacks, creating an additional three craters in the ground as well as more dead Nairabians.

The Nairabian archery brigade located at the rear of the two footmen brigades, which consisted of about a thousand, armed bowmen, had finally moved close enough to be within shooting range. The archery brigade commander immediately ordered the first Nairabian volley of the battle.

"Incoming!" a Horack archer on the wall yelled as the Nairabian arrows rained down on them.

Many Horack archers, as well as a few Horack footmen on the inside of the city wall, were hit by arrows, in addition to a handful of accidental Nairabian footmen caught in the crossfire. One of the casualties was the newly promoted Dathen Battle Mage Nicolas Dunheimer, who was struck with an arrow through his left bicep. Dathen Dunheimer fell to the ground with the rest of his fellow Dathens and soldiers who managed to react quick enough to duck behind the raised ledge of the defense wall.

"You alright, Dunheimer?" Dathen Battle Mage Lucas Chaims asked.

Dathen Battle Mage Dunheimer simply winced in response. Dathen Vangoff joined the conversation. "Look, I'm going to need you to try to continue the fight. Here, let me help you." Dathen Vangoff proceeded to snap both the fletching end as well as the arrow tip end from the main arrow body of the arrow that was stuck in his teammate's arm. Now just a small bit of arrow remained in Dathen Dunheimer's arm.

"Come on, friend," Dathen Chaims spoke. "Let's go."

All three Dathens stood up just as the Horack archers had finished returning their own volley of arrows.

"Let's take out the archers this time," Dathen Vangoff ordered the other Dathens.

Both Dathen Vangoff and Dathen Chaims once again prepared for another Blast Spell. Unfortunately, Dathen Dunheimer struggled to do the same, for he was unable to fully extend his left arm due to the persistent pain from his arrow wound. Not to mention the pain also made it difficult for him to concentrate. Dathen Dunheimer, through winces and gritted teeth, continued his attempt to perform the spell. Dathen Vangoff's, as well as Dathen Chaims' Blast Spells went off without issue. However, Dathen Dunheimer wasn't so lucky. His spell failed to cast so miserably from its poor execution, that it literally blew up in his face. Fortunately for those around him, the weakened spell wasn't strong enough to harm anyone close by. Unfortunately for Dathen Dunheimer, it was still strong enough to knock him clear off the wall and to his death below.

Dathen Vangoff and Dathen Chaims didn't have time to mourn their partner's unexpected passing. They had no choice but to continue blasting the Nairabian horde as much as possible. Besides, if everything went right, they knew he'd be back the next morning with a veteran status like the two of them.

Dathen Vangoff and Dathen Chaims, along with the help of the archers present on the wall, managed to decimate a large portion of the Nairabian archery brigade. Unfortunately, this left the Nairabian archers so defeated by their Horack enemies that they were forced to draw out their short swords and join the other two footmen brigades.

The remaining Nairabian brigades made it through the wall as the two armies were quickly reaching a stalemate. The Horack archers turned their attention to shooting the Nairabian footmen below, who all had shifted their turtle shields from above their heads, to in front of them. This, unfortunately for them, left their heads exposed to the incoming Horack arrows from above. Unfortunately for Dathen Vangoff and Dathen Chaims, it was no longer safe for them to use their Blast Spells and had to think of some other way to inflict damage on their enemies.

Losing morale, the Horack footmen on the ground began to retreat into the city center, with many of the Nairabians following them. One of the Nairabian footmen made an attempt to climb the ladder leading to the top of the wall, where the two surviving Dathen Battle Mages and the remaining Horack archers were. Fortunately for the Horacks, Dathen Battle Mage Vangoff saw the attempt to scale the wall and swiftly kicked the ladder to the ground, which ceased the advance. Unfortunately, this action also cut off Dathen Vangoff's and his fellow Horacks' most easily accessible route off the wall.

"Come on!" Dathen Vangoff yelled to anyone on the wall within earshot of him, "We've got to find another way down!"

Dathen Chaims and more than a dozen other archers immediately followed Dathen Vangoff down the wall walkway to find another way off. Slowly, all the others on the wall in the vicinity of Dathen Vangoff who weren't close enough to hear him give the order to move saw everyone else moving in one direction and followed as well, despite not knowing where they were going or why. They eventually came to the next warning bell tower a good way down. There they were able to use the bell tower ladder to climb down. However, the two Dathens and their band of archers weren't the first ones to the ladder. The non-local soldier reinforcements from the funeral were advancing towards the battle – freshly armed with weapons supplied by the Tenton Keep armory.

Dathen Vangoff slid down the ladder as quickly as possible to meet them on the ground.

"Hold up!" he spoke to them. "Our men are on the run and are likely headed to The Temple. Let's head that way and meet them. Let's join our brothers and sisters there and try to turn the tide of the battle in our favor while we still can!"

Chapter 11

Temple Defense

Dathen Vangoff was right in his assumption that the retreating soldiers would head to The Temple to regroup. However, whether that proved to be a wise decision or not had still yet to be determined. Located at The Temple was the other three remaining Horack Dathens, who, together, far outnumbered the two Nairabian Dathens on site. However, this also meant that all of the still living Horack Dathens would all be together in one convenient location. If all five of the remaining Horack Dathens were to die in this battle, it would prove catastrophic for the Horack nation.

When what was left of the two Horack brigades, commanded by Colonel Robert Therman and Colonel Cypher Tames, arrived at The Temple, the pyre that once contained the body of the deceased Dathen Lord was still burning brightly. Dathen Guardians Jasmine Blanes and Mortagart Milstrum, as well as Dathen Lord George Grook, were fortunately nowhere to be seen, not that anyone was surprised by their absence. They had done the wise thing and sought shelter inside The Temple itself. Even more fortunate for the Horacks on site, the Horack militia, commanded by Anthony Jenkins, had retrieved and readied their weapons from their homes and had rendezvoused back at The Temple, ready to fight their Nairabian enemies. The weapons the militia carried mostly consisted of a random assortment of different swords, bow and arrows, and makeshift spears, as well as some more unconventional weapons, like blacksmithing hammers.

Many of the surviving Horack regulars were immediately relieved to see the militia as potential reinforcements. The two Horack brigades stopped short of the burning pyre and turned around to face their Nairabian enemies once more. The militia force, led by Anthony Jenkins at the front, too charged forward around to the front of the pyre. Together, the two half-sized brigades, as well as the militia force, created a wall blocking the pyre. Each force shared the same idea of trying to protect their cremating dignitary from potentially being disrespected by the advancing Nairabians.

The two nations clashed once more into a fray of swords and other assorted weapons. Every Horack on site fought with all their hearts to drive back the Nairabian invasion. Even the Horack militia were seen giving it their all, who after spending their entire lives never setting foot on the battlefield, were very excited to finally play a combat role in the war that had been going on since any of them could remember. However, despite their excitement for battle and their twelve years of military training under Anthony Jenkins, their lack of real-world combat experience on the battlefield had shown through. The militia force in the middle of the two professionally trained Horack brigades began to quickly dwindle at a faster rate than their Horack military counterparts to their left and right.

Dathen Hector Vangoff and Dathen Lucas Chaims arrived at the reignited battle just minutes after it began. Fortunately for them, the archers and the footmen that followed them there had their presence go completely unnoticed by the two feuding armies. This gave them more than plenty of time to launch a surprise attack. The mass of assorted soldiers who had followed the two Dathen Battle Mages, immediately charged into the fray of Nairabian soldiers and Horack nationals without being ordered to do so.

There, both Dathen Vangoff and Dathen Chaims stood, alone, as the soldiers who had been with them just a short while ago, joined the skirmish. Both Dathens drew out their issued longswords and prepared for battle. In a moment of solidarity, Dathen Vangoff lightly punched Dathen Chaims on the shoulder and began to move towards the fight, but Dathen Chaims stopped him.

"Wait, sir. I have an idea," Dathen Chaims spoke.

Dathen Vangoff stopped and looked at Dathen Chaims to show that he had his attention.

"Watch," Dathen Chaims spoke again.

Then, Dathen Chaims reached into his satchel of magic sand and pulled out a handful of the magic material, just like he had already done so many times during the battle, and began to speak an incantation for a new spell. The magic sand component began to glow blue, just like it would for any other spell, but this time it also gained a paste-like consistency, similar to the time Dathen Vangoff created an Acid Spell to help defeat a Nairabian footman at the Battle of Rogue's Mountain Keep. While still speaking the proper incantation, Dathen Chaims began to rub the gelatinous sand onto the blade of his drawn weapon, and it immediately began to adhere itself to the blade. Dathen Vangoff, realizing what spell in their arsenal his partner was conducting, pulled out a handful of sand from his own satchel as well and began the process of preparing the same spell.

The two Dathens continued the process of rubbing the paste-like sand on their weapons, until their blades were completely covered. Once they were satisfied with the amount of coverage they had obtained, both Dathens paused to look at each other. Then almost in unison, they both turned their attention back to their sand-paste covered weapons to speak the final necessary word in their Dathen language to complete the spell. Almost simultaneously, both of the Dathen blades emitted a flash of bright, blue light. After the second it took for the flash of blue light to clear, it was revealed that the sand-paste that had been adhered to their weapons had disappeared and now their weapons were giving off more of a lightning-like effect.

Both Dathens raised their blue-electrified longswords in the air and both struck down the nearest Nairabian enemies they could find. Along with each blade easily cutting a massive slice into their respective targets, they also did electric shock damage to their enemies.

The areas of the bodies that each Nairabian was struck, seemed to immediately convulse uncontrollably. There could also be seen very faint puffs of smoke emanating from the bodies. Fortunately for the two Dathens, and unfortunately for any nearby Nairabians, this spell wasn't a one and done spell. One cast of the spell yielded about four to six good charges before the magic finally wore off. Both of the unfortunate Nairabian warriors fell to the ground, still convulsing, until they eventually died from their injuries.

Both Dathen Vangoff and Dathen Chaims made their ways through the Nairabian lines, striking down and electrifying unfortunate targets as they went. Dathen Chaims spotted his next potential target that needed electrifying. Although, he was a bit disturbed by the appearance of the newest Nairabian fighter to enter his vicinity. This new opponent didn't look like your average Nairabian. He was tall and muscular enough to be a

Nairabian, but aside from that, he had a very grotesque appearance. The Nairabian's most notable feature was a moderately long cut wound that spanned diagonally across his bare chest. This wound wasn't caused by the edge of a Horack sword that the Nairabian failed to block or get out of the way of. No. This wound was self-inflicted by the Nairabian himself. This man, who was known as 'Footman Drano', believed that self-inflicted wounds made him more intimidating on the battlefield. Aside from the fresh wound on his chest, a half dozen or so old wounds could also still be seen scattered throughout the exposed portions of his body. These old wounds were just as self-inflicted as the one on his chest, but had long since scarred over. With the nature of the Dathen magic being the way it was, any and all cuts and nicks sustained in a battle would heal naturally and remain visible on the body until the wearer was fully killed in combat and brought back again. This meant that Footman Drano's scars were a clear indication that he had spent a lot of time in battle since his last time visiting the Nairabian's version of 'The Dream State'.

 Footman Drano gave Dathen Chaims an animalistic grin, before charging at him. Both Dathen Chaims and Drano's swords collided together, blocking each other's attacks. Unfortunately for Drano, Dathen Chaims' sword still had the lightning enchantment casted upon it and Drano's of course didn't. Electrical energy quickly traveled down Drano's blade and shocked his hand, causing him to instinctively drop his sword. Drano looked around for another plan of attack. Then, Drano saw an opening in the militia force that would allow him access to the still burning pyre. Drano quickly ran towards the pyre and picked up a still burning log. Dathen Chaims, visibly angered by his target being so close to his fallen Dathen Lord, ran after him.

Drano swung around the flaming log he had picked up, like a club.

Drano made multiple attempts to club Dathen Chaims in the head, or across the face, but Dathen Chaims managed to successfully dodge each attack, until one attempt knocked Dathen Chaims' sword right out of his hand. This hit also managed to simultaneously cut Drano's burning log in half in the process, sending bits of burning log and embers everywhere. Both Drano and Dathen Chaims stood weaponless, but Drano still had his turtle shield to fight with.

Dathen Chaims knew the only way he was going to defeat his Nairabian opponent was to fight dirty. Dathen Chaims put both his hands up and prepared to fight with his fists. Dathen Chaims bobbed left and right, trying to figure out his next plan of action. Unfortunately, he didn't have much time to think, because he suddenly saw Drano charging at him with his turtle shield out, ready to smash into him. Dathen Chaims quickly lunged to the left to get out of the charging warrior's way. The momentum of Drano's charge drove him right past Dathen Chaims by several feet. This gave Dathen Chaims the opportunity to strike. The Dathen lunged at the distracted Nairabian's back and landed a right hook into the back of Drano's left abdomen.

Drano stopped his charge and turned around to face his opponent once more. Dathen Chaims' may have been the first one to land a hit in the fight, but unarmed combat was still a skill he had very little training in, and he desperately wanted to find any item he could use as a weapon. Then it occurred to him. He still had his satchel that contained the magic sand that was a vital ingredient in all his spells. Now, it was true that Dathen Chaims simply didn't have enough time to use it for any of his spells, but maybe he could find another use for it. Dathen Chaims removed the satchel from across his body and heaved it at Drano's head. Drano, ready for the attack, instinctively leaned his body back to dodge it, but that was exactly what Dathen Chaims wanted him to do. Dathen Chaims knew that by leaning back to dodge it, Drano would have to shift his hips and torso forward just a bit, as well as temporarily obscure Drano's vision long enough for Dathen Chaims to land an unobstructed hit. That's when Dathen Chaims landed a swift kick to Drano's groin. Dathen Chaims hated fighting with such a cheap attack, but he had to do what he had to do to survive. Drano groaned from the pain in his crotch. Drano was angered by Dathen Chaims landing two successful hits, while he hadn't landed any yet, especially with the last one hitting such a sensitive area. Drano removed his turtle shield from his arm and gripped it with both his hands. He then charged right at Dathen Chaims, with his shield raised high in the air – ready to strike. Drano struck the unfortunate Dathen in the head with his shield, knocking the Dathen out cold.

Drano grabbed the knocked out Dathen by the collar and lifted him to his feet. Drano then immediately made a fist with his right hand and slammed it hard into Dathen Chaims' face, easily breaking his nose. Dathen Chaims was completely helpless to fend for himself. A couple of more slams from Drano's superiorly larger firsts, connected to superiorly stronger arms, and it was all over for the helpless Dathen. Dathen Chaims was dead just a few seconds later.

The Nairabian Dathen Battle Mage known as 'Marcus Grundan' had been there to witness the death of the Horack Dathen, Lucas Chaims. Dathen Grundan smiled at the sight of yet another Horack Dathen falling. However, his savoring of the moment was short-lived when he felt a sharp pain in his lower back, followed by hot electricity coursing through his torso. Dathen Grundan had been skewered in the back by Dathen Vangoff. Dathen Vangoff, having fought against other Nairabian Dathens before, knew exactly how to exploit the scale mail armor they routinely wore into battle. Dathen Vangoff was sure to make his attack an upward jab, to increase his chances of landing the tip of his blade up under the scales and into the weak points of the armor.

Even more unfortunate for the Nairabian Dathen, was that the Armor Spell he had casted on himself prior to the battle had worn off after enough damage had been dealt to Dathen Grundan, from previous opponents he had fought earlier in the battle. The Dathen Armor Spell was only good for up to twenty-four hours after the spell had been casted, in which case it would just naturally wear off, or until enough damage had been done to the wearer to break the spell.

Dathen Vangoff wasn't able to penetrate as deeply as he would have if the Dathen hadn't been wearing any armor at all, but the metallic armor did also prove to be Dathen Grundan's weakness. The metal in the armor was conductive enough that the electricity that was still coursing through Dathen Vangoff's sword was able to send electric shocks into Dathen Grundan's torso. Dathen Grundan fell down onto the cobble stone ground, and had stopped convulsing from the electric shock the moment Dathen Vangoff's sword left his body. Dathen Vangoff then rolled the Nairabian Dathen over on his back with his foot, so that he could look his opponent in the eye before killing him. Dathen Vangoff took barely a second to savor the moment before plunging his longsword, which had since run out of electricity from the last hit, into Dathen Grundan's neck, killing him.

Next, Dathen Vangoff desperately wanted to kill the

grotesque warrior who had killed his friend and partner. He charged towards Drano, but another Nairabian soldier had stepped in front of his path, blocking him from his intended target, but Dathen Vangoff was able to easily strike him down without issue. As soon as the Nairabian soldier was neutralized, Dathen Vangoff looked up once more to see where Drano had moved to, but he had completely disappeared from sight. Dathen Vangoff didn't have time to curse his luck, for another Nairabian warrior stepped into the Dathen's view, wanting to fight. He too, was easily neutralized like the other one before him. Dathen Vangoff continued to slay any Nairabians who came his way, hoping to have a chance to cross paths again with the grotesque warrior who had killed his friend.

Chapter 12

One Step Backwards and Two Steps Forward

Despite the close proximity of everyone involved in the close quarters combat, Nairabian Dathen Battle Mage Vincent Brody was completely unaware that his Dathen partner had just perished at the hands of a Horack Dathen. Although, it didn't matter, because Dathen Brody still had a second part of his mission to complete. The first part was to help blow a large enough sized hole into the Tenton defense wall, and the second part was to blow up as much of the Tenton Temple as he could. Dathen Brody readied another Blast Spell, just like he had done before when he was still outside the Horack capital.

Dathen Brody launched the explosive ball of sand directly at one of the two square buildings that made up the religious complex. This also happened to be the same square building that Enron had come out of just a few days prior, when he was brought back from The Dream State for the first time. The casted spell easily blasted away a third of the building, rumbling the ground as it exploded.

***

Inside an underground chamber, inside The Temple complex, Dathen Lord George Grook, along with Dathen Guardians Mortagart Milstrum and Jasmine Blanes waited. Waited for the battle to be over, waited for instruction, just waited for some kind of action that would require them to leave their safe haven. Then, BOOM! the ground, walls, and even the ceiling shook from the explosion caused by Dathen Brody. The three high-ranking Dathens looked up at the ceiling, concerned.

Dathen Grook gave a deep sigh. "The battle has moved deep inside the city," he spoke. "Milstrum, Blanes," he continued. "Go up to the surface and see how we're fairing and help out as needed."

"Yes, sir!" Dathen Guardian Blanes answered her boss.

However, Dathen Milstrum was hesitant to immediately obey his superior's order. "And you're going to stay here, sir?" Dathen Milstrum asked Dathen Grook.

"Of course, Milstrum." Dathen Grook answered him

"And you're not going to be coming up to the surface until this is all over, correct? Sir," Dathen Milstrum continued.

"Yes! Milstrum!" Dathen Grook barked.

Dathen Milstrum knew all too well about how Dathen Grook missed his days as a Battle Mage and knew there would be a chance he would be tempted to join in the fight. However, he knew it would be in their best interest for him to stay where he was.

***

Jasmine and Mortagart climbed a spiral staircase that led up to the surface level. They exited The Temple through the rectangular main building of the complex. Outside The Temple, the two Dathen Guardians were able to fully grasp the magnitude of the battle. They had seen combat before, during their times as Battle Mages, and they normally wouldn't be phased by such a sight, but this scene particularly horrified them. That was because neither one of them had ever seen combat this close to home before. However, the two of them knew they had to put their emotions aside and put themselves back into that combat mindset once more.

"You ready for this?" Dathen Milstrum asked his partner, somewhat rhetorically.

"Am I ready for this?" Dathen Blanes repeated. "Please! Remember, I was still fighting on the front lines of this war up until a few days ago. So really, I should be asking you, 'are *you* ready for this?', old man," Dathen Blanes teased her partner.

Both Dathen Milstrum and Dathen Blanes heard another explosion and felt the ground rumble once more, except this time it was louder and stronger than the one they felt and heard while underground. They both immediately looked up to see Dathen Brody readying yet another Blast Spell. Dathen Milstrum had been away from combat for nearly six years, and since then he had become an expert at the Dathen Resurrection Spell, but also in that time he had become quite rusty at performing most of the Dathen's combat-oriented spells. However, the one spell he still hadn't forgotten how to perform, was easily their most commonly used combat spell, and was the same spell Nairabian Dathen Brody was using to destroy their precious temple: the Blast Spell.

Dathen Milstrum readied a Blast Spell with the intent on taking out the Nairabian Dathen, except this time, he intentionally grabbed a smaller handful of sand than he normally would have used for the spell. Enough of their city had already been destroyed by Dathen Brody, and Dathen Milstrum wanted to continue to minimize further damage to the city as much as possible, especially since he was aiming for a singular target.

Dathen Milstrum readied his spell as quickly as possible, but he wasn't quick enough. Dathen Brody was able to complete one final Blast spell and completely destroy the square building, leaving nothing but a crater where it once was.

Dathen Brody was admiring his work just as he heard the mild rumbling, trademark sound of a Blast spell coming his way. He was able to look up in time to see a golf ball sized version of the spell careening towards him. Noticing the spell too late, Dathen Brody was unable to get out of its path quick enough. With a deer in the headlights expression, Dathen Brody exploded into about two dozen pieces.

Dathen Milstrum drew out his longsword and looked at his partner, who had also drawn her weapon. They both gave a fist bump with their non-bladed hands, and walked into the fray, hacking down Nairabian grunts with ease as they went. Although Dathen Blanes had a slightly easier time defeating Nairabian enemies than her partner, Dathen Milstrum was still able to hold his own despite his six-year absence from the battlefield. Dathen Milstrum managed to strike down no less than ten enemies and send them all to their own version of The Dream State, before a more formidable enemy entered his line of sight. It was the grotesque warrior, Footman Drano, looking to add another Horack Dathen casualty to his list of kills.

Dathen Milstrum gave the same surprised expression that Footman Drano seemed to cause all people upon their first time meeting him. Dathen Milstrum readied his sword and prepared to attack, but Drano was just as quick to launch his own attack with his new scimitar that he had acquired from one of his fallen buddies. The Nairabian scimitar and the Horack longsword clanged together into a parry. Drano prepared for another attack, but Dathen Milstrum was ready for that one too. Drano sliced down diagonally at the Dathen, but Dathen Milstrum managed to jump back, avoiding it. However, the Nairabian blade did manage to skim off the surface of the Dathen's chainmail shirt, causing minor damage to the metal rings, but leaving the Dathen completely unharmed. Drano continued to swipe at Dathen Milstrum, making an X pattern with his scimitar, putting Dathen Milstrum on a backward stepping retreat. Dathen Milstrum knew he had to do something to gain the upper hand. Dathen Milstrum ducked low and charged under Drano's guard, stabbing him in his unprotected torso.

***

Mortagart wasn't the only Milstrum still alive on the battlefield at the time, killing their fair share of Nairabian invaders. Mortagart's son, Enron had managed to survive at least till this point in the battle, and had even killed a couple of Nairabians along the way. For Enron, this fight was the polar opposite of how his first combat experience had turned out. Enron was no longer timid on the battlefield, now that he had died once before, visited The Dream State, and come back again.

Enron saw his father battling the strange warrior, just as Dathen Milstrum was pulling his blade from Drano's gut. Enron, wanting to aid his father, ran towards the beast to launch a surprise attack at the unsuspecting soldier. Dathen Milstrum suddenly took notice of his son's presence and was momentarily distracted. Drano took advantage of the Dathen's distraction and moved his scimitar into a low, horizontal slice. Drano cut straight through Dathen Milstrum's neck, completely decapitating him.

"Nooo!" Enron screamed at the beast.

Filled with rage after seeing his father die right before his eyes, Enron went berserk and charged at Drano with his round shield up and his sword edge pointed straight at the warrior. Drano heard the enraged Horack coming for him and turned around to fight him too. However, Drano was no match for someone of the emotional state that had just seen their father murdered. Enron skewered Drano through the abdomen, before Drano could even fully turn around to fight. Enron's sword landed mere inches from the same wound his father had left seconds earlier, but Enron wasn't done with his father's killer. Enron dropped his olive green round shield, grabbed the hilt of his sword with both hands, and moved the blade sideways to the right. The blade ripped through Drano's intestines until the blade popped free on the other side of him, spilling some of Drano's guts as it went.

Footman Drano's death didn't satisfy Enron's rage. He desperately looked around for another victim to kill. Enron struck down another unfortunate Nairabian, and then another, and another. Five, six, seven more Nairabians were hacked down without mercy. That's when Enron's rage began to wear off and his muscles started to exhaust. Enron stood in the middle of the killing fields that was once his city's Temple, panting heavily. Enron stood in a state of euphoria, taking in the situation around him, until he felt a sharp, yet familiar pain in his side. While trying to take a break from his rage-induced massacre, Enron had completely missed the Nairabian warrior who came up from behind and stabbed him in his right side. Enron groaned from the stab wound, but he mostly accepted that this was going to be his end for this battle. Enron had avenged his father's death, and that was good enough for him. Now Enron just looked forward to seeing his father again in The Dream State. Enron didn't have to wait long, for the same warrior who stabbed his side, had since removed his blade and used it to decapitate Enron, the same way his father had been killed.

Both father and son had died within a minute of each other. Enron's killer on the other hand, didn't have time to celebrate another death being added to his growing kill count. Archer Ester, the soldier Enron had befriended at The Battle of Sickle Ridge, had put an end to his friend's killer with a quick slice to their intestines.

There had been many Horack lives lost in the struggle to defend their Temple. A couple of the lives lost that were considered to be of particularly high value included a Dathen Guardian and a Dathen Battle Mage – two Dathen Battle Mages if you count Dathen Battle Mage Dunheimer who died at the wall from a poorly executed Blast spell. Colonel Cypher Tames, the commander of one of the brigades of professionally trained soldiers had also lost his life, as well as Anthony Jenkins, the militia commander, and finally, Grand Marshal Baker wasn't able to survive the battle either, leaving Deputy Grand Marshal Stalls in command of the Horack army.

Despite all their losses, the Horacks had vanquished both Nairabian Dathens that had shown up to battle – leaving no other Nairabian-friendly Dathens on site – as well as vanquished Footman Drano, possibly the scariest soldier the Nairabians had in their ranks. For all this, the Horacks had the Nairabians on the run. Possibly soon, the Nairabians would be chased once more through the hole in the defense wall they came from, and out of the city. Then, this traumatic day for the Horack people could finally be over.

Chapter 13

On the Run

Dathen Guardian Jasmine Blanes sprinted down the spiral staircase to inform her boss that the Nairabians were on the run, but also that his second-in-command had died in the process. Dathen Lord George Grook sighed after hearing about Dathen Milstrum's passing.

"Well," he began. "It'll be alright. We'll see him again soon enough. Now, let's show our enemies what happens when you're dumb enough to invade our city!"

"Sir, do you mean to join in the fight?" Dathen Blanes asked her boss.

"Of course!" he replied. "There is no way I'm going to miss killing a few Nairabians in a battle that is surely ours."

Dathen Blanes was uncomfortable with the idea of Dathen Lord Grook coming out of his safe haven, but he did have a point, the battle was almost surely theirs. Also, Dathen Blanes had always been somewhat intimidated by Dathen Grook's aggressive demeanor and didn't want to argue with him.

Dathen Guardian Blanes ascended the spiral staircase once more, with Dathen Lord Grook shortly behind her. What they saw upon exiting The Temple didn't surprise Dathen Blanes, for she had already witnessed the devastation the battle had taken on their precious Temple, but the sight absolutely horrified Dathen Lord Grook. It wasn't the piles of bodies consisting of both

Horacks and Nairabians that were scattered everywhere that horrified him. It was seeing that one of their buildings, which had once been a part of The Temple complex, had been reduced to nothing but a crater, was what disturbed him the most. Also, Dathen Lord Grook managed to spot the headless body of his next-in-command, Dathen Guardian Mortagart Milstrum. Dathen Lord Grook was of course already aware of his fallen friend, but it didn't fully sink in until he laid eyes on the body itself. Dathen Lord Grook did well with keeping his anger and disgust to himself as they advanced on the heels of the Horack regulars and militia, that didn't hesitate to chase down the retreating Nairabian invaders.

The Nairabians hit the Tenton defense wall and were immediately faced with the same funnel effect they experienced at the start of the battle. The Nairabians who weren't fortunate enough to make it through the opening first, were forced to turn around and fight off the Horack front while they waited for their turn. Once again, Dathen Hector Vangoff could be seen at the front of the advance, continuing to fight more than his fair share of Nairabians. However, his participation in the battle since its conception proved to be too much for him. After almost two hours of continuous fighting, Dathen Vangoff's muscles began to exhaust and his strikes began to become sloppy and poorly executed. It was Dathen Vangoff's second visit to the Tenton defense wall that day and that was where he met his end. He was hit in the side by a Nairabian's scimitar as he was trying to block another Nairabian's incoming attack.

Dathen Lord Grook was completely unaware of yet another one of his colleagues' passing. He was far too busy holding his own inside the fray to have noticed. In an almost macabre way, Dathen Grook was filled with glee as he hacked down Nairabian after Nairabian. It's not that Dathen Lord Grook particularly enjoyed killing people, it was more of a feeling of nostalgia that filled the Dathen leader, who had been away from the battlefield for nearly a decade. Dathen Jasmine Blanes on the other hand, fought with no real emotion of any kind. For her, it was just another day of fighting her Nairabian enemies.

The dozen or so Horack archers who happened to still be alive and managed to survive against the Nairabians thus far scaled the defense wall once more – back to their original fighting positions. They once again traded out their short swords for their primary bow and arrow weapons. They were expecting to get the opportunity to fire down on the Nairabian invaders as they fled their city, but from atop the wall, they saw something they weren't expecting. A fresh brigade of Nairabian troops had appeared on the horizon and were marching for their city. It was General Wainwright's brigade that had finally shown up to the battle.

Their unexpected delay at the Battle of Sickle Ridge, as well as their further north starting position, caused their arrival to Tenton to take longer than they had originally expected. Now that they had finally arrived, the Horack's certain victory didn't seem so certain anymore. Also, the meager number of archers still available on the wall were not enough to launch much of a preemptive attack against the fresh troops. Worse yet, all of the ballista crew members had already fallen in battle and there was nobody left alive who could properly operate the artillery weapons. Without proper artillery support, the handful of archers left alive had no chance of even making an attempt at defeating the advancing Testudo formation. The Horack archers also remained leaderless, with all their commanders and sergeants being slain in battle. This also included their impromptu leader,

Dathen Vangoff, being gone as well. The leaderless archers just stood around, not really sure what to do

"You!" one of the archers spoke, grabbing another archer by the shoulder. It was Archer Ester who broke the silence, "The troops on the ground are going to need to know about the additional threat coming from beyond our wall. Go run to the nearest warning bell tower and ring it with all of your might," Archer Ester instructed him.

The archer nodded at the order and quickly ran off to execute the command.

"For the rest of us," Archer Ester spoke once more. "The Nairabians on the ground are not likely expecting an attack from above, and therefore are still vulnerable to an arrow attack. Let's take a few of them out while we wait for the warning bell."

The archers did as they were instructed, aiming their bows over the ledge of the damaged defense wall and firing at the Nairabians below. A number of Nairabians equal to the number of arrows fired, fell from the attack.

"Ding, ding, ding!" About two-hundred meters away from the archers, the nearest intact warning bell rang out under the operation of the instructed archer.

Archer Ester smiled at the quickness and the success of the warning bell ring. Now that the bell had been rung, it was only a matter of time before people would start to scale the wall to investigate. Fortunately, Archer Ester didn't have to wait long for his first investigator to come. It was Dathen Lord Grook who had grown curious of the situation and joined the archers on the wall.

"What is this meaning of this?" Dathen Lord Grook began to say, as he neared the top of the ladder, but the answer he was looking for came to him as soon as his line of sight cleared the top of the wall.

Dathen Grook paused for a moment to take in the situation, as well as come up with a plan to deal with the unexpected guests. Dathen Grook reached into his bag of magic sand and prepared a Fireball spell. With the quickness of an experienced Dathen, the Fireball spell was ready to be thrown. Dathen Lord Grook launched the ball of fire directly at the main formation of Nairabian reinforcements, and they were immediately engulfed in flames. Although, there was something special about this Fireball spell, because it was complete with additional magical properties that ensured its fire would adhere to anything it touched. In the case of the fresh Nairabian troops, it was mostly their turtle shell shields, which they held up to make their Testudo formation. Any of the turtle shell shields that were caught in the area of effect immediately caught fire and soon became too hot for the Nairabians to continue to hold; thus, it forced them to drop them. The dropped Nairabian turtle shields then opened the Nairabians themselves to be exposed to the flames of the fireball. Any Nairabians caught in the spell's area of effect soon caught fire as well, becoming the first Nairabian casualties of the new attack wave.

The burning Nairabians screamed and wailed, creating sounds that could only come from someone who was literally on fire! The remaining Nairabians who survived the fireball attack, not wanting to experience the same horrific fate as their unfortunate friends, took flight and charged for the Tenton defense wall.

Eager for battle, as well as wanting to make their presence known to their struggling friends, the Nairabian reinforcements literally pushed themselves into the mass of soldiers, further pushing them back inside Tenton.

"Come on! Move, you cowards!" a Nairabian reinforcement

yelled.

"Get back in there!" shouted another.

With their moral raising, the remainder of the Nairabians troops who had initiated the battle a couple of hours earlier began to push back against their Horack enemies. The battle for Tenton had been reignited once more.

Dathen Lord Grook cursed himself for not reacting fast enough and popping off more spells before the reinforcements could enter the city. Dathen Grook slid down the same ladder he had climbed earlier and rejoined the battle below. The Dathen leader quickly struck down a number of Nairabian intruders with his longsword without issue. Unfortunately, he was so engrossed in the nostalgia of the battle, that he was completely unaware that Dathen Blanes had made her way through the lines and joined his side. Furthermore, his blind longing for the battlefield allowed him to completely forget that there were still only two Horack Dathens left alive, including himself.

Dathen Blanes continued to hold her own on the battlefield while simultaneously trying to get her boss's attention. Finally, seeing enough of a lull in the battle, Dathen Blanes was able to toss her longsword to her left hand, thus, freeing up her dominant hand to grab Dathen Grook's shoulder and speak.

"Sir! We really should go. Your life is far too important to be out here in all this chaos. Arguably, my life is too important to be out here as well, but yours especially," Dathen Blanes pleaded with him.

Dathen Grook looked at his subordinate for a very short second, long enough to realize she was right. Dathen Grook quickly noticed an incoming Nairabian attack and shot his sword up to block it and followed it with a counterattack, killing his latest assailant. "Oh, alright." He sighed. "I guess I've had enough fun for today."

Dathen Grook and Dathen Blanes both made a backward stepping retreat out of the fray, blocking enemy attacks as they went. That was until Dathen Grook felt something grab his leg. It was a fallen Nairabian warrior that he had defeated earlier. The fallen soldier laid bleeding, clearly not fit enough to continue fighting, but not quite dead yet. The fallen Nairabian wasn't trying to trip Dathen Grook or anything like that. In fact, the fallen Nairabian wasn't even aware of which alliance the leg belonged to that he grabbed. All he knew was he had ahold of someone's leg and it might have been his only chance to pick himself back up again. Regardless of the dying Nairabian's actual intentions, the sudden leg grip caused Dathen Grook to topple backwards, onto the dying Nairabian.

Dathen Grook laid on the dying warrior, frantically trying to get back up, as more enemies closed in around him. Dathen Blanes reached out for him with her free hand, but was forced to quickly retract it again as she spotted an incoming attack aimed at slicing her reaching hand from her body. With the attack successfully dodged, she quickly switched her weapon back from her left hand, into her dominant hand again to quickly dispose of the source of the unfriendly gesture.

Dathen Grook looked up to see three Nairabian footmen advancing on him. Dathen Grook started to realize the gravity of his mistake to have left The Temple safe haven. Dathen Grook knew there was little chance of him defeating all three of the advancing enemies, even with the aid of Dathen Blanes, who was fighting off her own enemies. Dathen Grook knew that if he was going to die, he was going to take at least one of them with him. Dathen Grook thrusted his longsword up, aimed for one his opponents' thighs, the only bit of exposed flesh Dathen Grook could spot that wasn't covered by the warrior's turtle shield. The warrior wailed in pain, but only temporarily, for the Nairabian was finally able to subsequently strike down the Dathen Lord with his scimitar.

Dathen Grook may have died, but before he went, his nearly two-hundred and thirty-pound body, if you include all his gear, had landed on the skull of the dying Nairabian he fell on earlier, killing him too. Unfortunately, Dathen Grook's death meant that Dathen Guardian Jasmine Blanes was the only Horack Dathen still standing.

Chapter 14

Peace at Last

The chaotic sounds of swords clashing, as well as fighters yelling and dying, was broken by the sound of a bugle suddenly playing. The bugle sound was to a tune that many of the Horack soldiers recognized. It was the designated song of 'surrender'. Slowly, and almost hesitantly, many of the Horack soldiers began to drop their weapons and put their hands up in the universal position of surrender, many of them dropping their heads in shame as they went. It started with the lower-ranking soldiers first, mostly those who had been to Warrior Hill recently and were the most familiar with the particular song. The more veteran soldiers did eventually join in their lower-ranking comrades, once they too remembered the meaning of the song.

The Nairabians, being honorable people, immediately recognized what the Horack soldiers were doing and honored it. Although, a handful of Horack soldiers were accidentally slain by Nairabian swords that couldn't be stopped in time for the sudden ceasing of the battle.

The bugle sound came from Lieutenant Jeffrey Jacobson, one of the members of Deputy Grand Marshal Stalls' entourage, under the order of the Deputy Grand Marshal himself. Deputy Grand Marshal Stalls had spent much of the battle in the background, doing his best to stay out of combat, especially after his predecessor had died. Seeing the Horack army struggle to defend their city and believing that all Horack Dathens had already died, Deputy Grand Marshal Stalls concluded the only logical course of action was to surrender to the Nairabians, in hopes of sparing the lives of all Horack people still standing.

The two armies stood in tense silence, especially the Horack army, who were mentally questioning the true level of honor their longtime enemies had, and were afraid that at any moment, the Nairabians would break their assumed truce and start slaughtering the then-unarmed Horacks once more.

The tense silence was finally broken by a series of Nairabian soldiers shouting the same phrase, "Make way! Make way!"

The frequency of the shouted phrase started out slowly and came from somewhere towards the back of the Nairabian army. Increasing in volume and frequency, soldiers at the front of the army began to move out of the way of someone trying to move to the front of the army. Finally, a female figure emerged from within the Nairabian ranks. It was General Natalie Wainwright, the highest-ranking Nairabian alive on the battlefield at the time. She was dressed in her scale mail armor and had since sheathed her bastard sword, and was resting her hand on the pommel of its hilt.

"Good. Now, these are our demands," she spoke with a soft, but firm voice. "First off, which one of you ordered the surrender?"

"I did," Deputy Grand Marshal Stalls spoke, who had been slowly pushing his way to the front of his own army, except no one in his army was calling to "Make way," like the Nairabians had done for their leader.

Instead, many of the soldiers within the Horack ranks immediately started entertaining thoughts of cruel violence against the military official, upon realizing it was him who ordered the surrender.

"Good," General Wainwright spoke again. "These are the demands I have been instructed by Grand Marshal Ratlin to carry out, upon seizing your city. You are to surrender all weapons, to include all tools and structures of war. This is to include your town keep, as well as your Dathen temple."

Many of the Horack soldiers gritted their teeth upon hearing the Nairabian demands, but Deputy Grand Marshal Stalls did what he did best, continued to show no emotion to the devastating news.

"These demands are to further include seizing of all towns, cities, bases, and other land properties belonging to the Horack nation, and holding a military presence in those locations until such a time that we deem it time to leave."

Deputy Grand Marshal Stalls waited an additional moment to hear what the general's other demands were, but she continued to remain silent for the time. "That's it?" the Deputy Grand Marshal asked, confused.

"That's it," she continued. "Follow these simple demands, and in exchange we will allow the rest of you to live. You can carry about your lives as you please, just without a standing military."

Deputy Grand Marshal Stalls, being the logical man that he was, realized that exchanging their military presence for the lives of the remaining Horack people was clearly the right answer. Deputy Grand Marshal Stalls walked towards the Nairabian general, stopping just within arm's reach of her. The Deputy Grand Marshal extended his hand and spoke, "Deal."

General Wainwright smiled as she shook the Horack's hand. She was pleased knowing it was her brigade that finally won the war.

Many of the Horacks who were still standing in their 'surrender' position sorrowfully closed their eyes in shame, knowing that they had been defeated.

"What about her, ma'am?" Dathen Battle Mage Saldore, the Dathen assigned to the General's brigade, asked his commander, while he pointed to Dathen Guardian Jasmine Blanes. General Wainwright took notice of the lone surviving Horack Dathen.

"Have her arrested," General Wainwright ordered without hesitation.

Two Nairabian footmen stepped out of the mass of troops to seize the woman.

"Over my dead body!" Dathen Blanes shouted as she picked up her dropped weapon once more. She quickly disposed of the two approaching Nairabian footmen who were somewhat caught off guard by her sudden attack. Five more Nairabian footmen broke from the group to make another attempt at taking her; this time they were prepared for a fight. Dathen Blanes screamed a cry of battle, showing her enemies she was not afraid of them. The clearly outmatched Dathen was able to take out another one of the footmen before the other four were able to slaughter the unfortunate woman.

General Wainwright shrugged her shoulders. "Dead works just as well too," she spoke completely nonchalantly.

"What about letting the rest of us live?" Deputy Grand Marshal Stalls shouted at the general, clearly angered by the sudden breaking of their assumed treaty.

"The rest of you will live as long as there are no more crazy outbursts. Got it?" General Wainwright answered him.

Deputy Grand Marshal Stalls looked over at the bloodied body of the final Horack Dathen to fall that day, thinking about how it would have been logical for her to just accept her arrest.

If she had done that, she would still be alive. Many of the Horack soldiers who were close enough to see the fallen Dathen also looked over at her and silently mourned her loss.

Deputy Grand Marshal Stalls looked back at the Nairabian general. "Fine. You won't have any more outbursts from us, ma'am. I promise."

***

Tenton had become a police state in the days that followed. Just as General Wainwright had said, the remainder of her brigade moved into the city and took it over. This included seizing the Horack's Dathen Temple.

For the Horacks that remained, they broke their tradition of cremating their dead, and instead buried the bodies in the city's first ever cemetery, which they placed just outside their city walls. Having lost access to their Dathen Temple, they weren't allowed to bring back those that had fallen in the battle. This meant that those Horacks who had been unfortunate enough to die in the battle for Tenton would likely never come back again. Although, the surviving members of Tenton couldn't just leave the bodies where they were to rot. Something had to be done with them. Therefore, burying them seemed like the most efficient option in such dire times.

The majority of those that were buried were put into mass graves, except for all six Dathens, as well as the Horack battle commanders who fell, including the militia commander, Anthony Jenkins, who each got their own individual graves for their deeds. Even Deputy Grand Marshal Stalls got his own grave, who was found in his bed with a dagger in his chest the morning after General Wainwright's takeover. Nobody ever discovered who the his assassin was. Although, Deputy Grand Marshal Stalls' decision to order the surrender of Tenton had proved to be an unpopular choice amongst the Horack people, so it could have essentially been anyone who killed him. Deputy Grand Marshal Stalls was given his own grave, not because the people of Tenton had a particular level of respect for him or felt he deserved a special place of honor, but because they didn't want to put him in any of the mass graves with the other soldiers and disrespect the true heroes of the battle. Not sure what else to do, they gave him his own unmarked grave away from everyone else's.

After Deputy Grand Marshal Stalls' death, Council President Henry Marquez took over as the designated leader of the Horack people. Signing an official treaty between the two nations was Council President Marquez's first act as the Horack ruler. Followed by that was the signing of several dozen copies of an official decree. The decree was to be used to inform the surrounding towns and bases inside the Horack nation that the war was over and the Horacks were to lay down their arms to make way for Nairabian control.

***

The time that followed the war was the closest thing to peace the two nations had experienced in nearly two-hundred years. After all, the two nations had never hated each other. Instead, they had always feared each other. They feared that if one nation had full control of the deity-given Dathens' powers, that nation would use them to devastate the other. That's what started the whole war in the first place. Fighting to be the army with full control of the power. This was each nation's only way to ensure they would not risk being the nation destroyed by the other.

Now that the outcome that both nations feared the most had happened, the Horacks began to realize there was never anything to fear from their longtime enemies. General Wainwright and the remainder of the Nairabian people kept their promise of allowing the Horack people to carry on as they pleased, just without a military presence. The city's merchants continued to sell goods as they pleased, like they always had. The Nairabian soldiers who took up a presence in the city didn't even demand any of the goods free of charge, as a way to pillage the city. The two nations were finally coexisting with each other as if they were longtime allies and not enemies.

The one-hundred and ninety-five-year war was finally over, but the real enemy of the two nations had still yet to be discovered...

To be continued in the next book: The 13th Dathen

Milton Keynes UK
Ingram Content Group UK Ltd.
UKHW010732160124
436122UK00001B/32